MW00654882

THE ALLEY

A murder mystery set on Vancouver Island

KATHY GARTHWAITE

THE BOOK FOLKS

Published by

The Book Folks

London, 2020

This book is a work of fiction. Names, characters, businesses, organizations, places and events are either the product of the author's imagination or are used fictitiously. Any resemblance to actual persons, living or dead, events or locales is entirely coincidental. The spelling is British English.

ISBN 978-1-913516-07-9

www.thebookfolks.com

For Daisy.

Chapter 1

Lorie Sanders hadn't shown up at her waitressing job for five days. Had something happened to her? More than likely she was another drifter who had rolled into town to make a few bucks during the peak summer season, and then left as quickly as she had arrived. No one seemed worried about the young lady except for her employer who had to work overtime to make up for the lost hours.

* * *

RCMP Sergeant Marlowe Flint sat in the Seabreeze Cafe on Main Street with nothing pressing on her agenda. It was one of the warmest days of the summer, so far. The restaurant was crowded, abuzz with the drone of voices, mostly from the tourists, and intermingled with the burst of giggles from the teenagers huddled in the back booths. From her seat, Flint had a view of the room from end to end.

She drank her coffee unhurriedly and fixed her gaze on Paula Wilkes, an old high school friend. The owner had a drawn face and tired eyes. At a call-out from the kitchen, she swung around to the pass-through window. The cafe was run the old-fashioned way, just like the owner. No computers or digital gadgets. Paula grabbed the plates that had been set on the open shelf and hustled to a couple sitting by the window.

The tinkle of a bell sounded softly. Half a dozen people glanced up as the entrance door swung open, heralded by a rush of warm air and a lone gentleman. The man strolled across the room to an empty stool at the end of the counter, his footfalls making no sound on the faded green linoleum. The worn tiles had a shiny look with a track ground down the middle from the countless shoes and boots over the decades. The customers returned to their conversations unconcerned by the slight distraction.

Flint took another sip of her coffee, almost ready to get back to work. But not quite. Her attention was drawn to the new arrival as he swivelled his stool back and forth lazily.

Of all the things from her childhood, the thing she envisioned best was the Saturday afternoon walks to this cafe with her mom, sitting on a tall stool made for adults, her skinny legs dangling in the air, chocolate milkshake moustache on her upper lip. All those simple days that seemed to go on forever, a pleasant thought.

Her own daughter was reaching the age when she would soon share the ritual and become part of the legacy. Paige would stroll down the street the same way Flint had, her tiny hand in her mother's comfortable grip, a faint tremble of doubt in the young child's mind, overcome by the excitement of the adventure.

The detective sighed. The move back to her hometown was the best thing she had done in a while. Although life had dealt her a recent blow, she felt reasonably good about things, settling into her new position at the Royal Canadian Mounted Police detachment in Castlecrest, British Columbia. As sergeant she headed the general investigation team consisting of a corporal, two constables and herself. They investigated the serious crimes of robbery, rape and murder.

Some gurgling squawks from the cappuccino machine gave advance warning to the ear-splitting sounds that would follow. All chatter stopped when the whistling from the steam wand hit an unbearable shriek. Paula turned down the dial, and the hissing stopped abruptly. In those few seconds of stillness, something – not a loud clap of thunder but the lesser, sharper crack of a whip – rang out.

Flint knew the sound.

She pushed her chair back, slopping the last of her coffee on the tabletop as she bumped it with her duty belt. She pressed her hand against her pistol to stop it from flapping against her hip as she ran outside, her boots hammering the floor with urgency. She paused momentarily on the landing to listen for another shot. None came. Browsers strolling along the sidewalk seemed impervious to the danger that was afoot. A fireman, Edward Ewert, appeared out of the crowd, heading toward her from the opposite direction.

"Hey, Teddy, did you see anyone?" Flint turned and looked at the fireman.

"No. I heard a shot and came running. I think it came from the jewelry store."

Flint swung toward Altman Jewelry and Diamonds that stood next to the cafe, its front entrance set back from the street. She pressed the button on her walkie-talkie and called for emergency backup. She didn't have long to wait. An unmarked cruiser pulled up tight to the curb. RCMP Corporal Naomi Thornberry jumped out and dashed up the stairs, breathing heavily, her face flushed. Her mother had told her she was big-boned, but really she was a few pounds overweight.

"What have we got?" Thornberry asked. She looked at the fireman and absently gave him a nod, unsure what he had to do with this.

"I don't know what's going on. I heard a single shot," Flint answered.

"Is it a robbery?"

"Well, there wasn't an alarm sent out but something bad happened. So let's take it slowly."

Flint drew her Smith & Wesson from its holster, holding it close to her body, her trigger finger along the frame of the gun. Thornberry followed suit, her body trembling slightly.

With her free hand, Flint turned the doorknob and pushed. She gripped her gun with both hands and extended her arms in front of her, prepared to take aim on a target.

"Police! Hands up!" she shouted into the opening.

There was no response. And no sounds.

She stepped into the shop and took a quick glance around an empty room that was longer than it was wide, with glass cases that extended along three of the perimeter walls.

Without turning, she gestured for the corporal to move in.

Flint advanced forward cautiously, both hands still on her weapon. Everything was gleaming inside and out. Except for a large broken glass cabinet and a pooling of dark liquid seeping from behind the case. She held up a closed fist to Thornberry and crept in closer.

A man sprawled out behind the long counter was covered with shattered glass shards. Several empty trays lined with velvet lay upturned, the diamonds scattered across the rustic pine flooring. There was a dark patch of blood on his light grey vest. She knelt on one knee at his side, hovered over the body to listen for breathing, and checked his pulse, looking for any sign at all that he was still alive. Flint stood up and shook her head. She skirted the wall as she moved toward the rear of the building, calling out as she went.

"Police! Is anybody there?"

Thornberry shadowed her into the room, keeping her weapon at the ready.

A door left ajar cast an eerie light into the dim hallway. Flint approached. She stood to the side and pushed on the partially open door. A florescent lamp on the desk glowed, but nobody was there. She passed two more doors, checking what might be hiding behind each. There was nothing amiss. Only a washroom and a closet.

Thornberry came in close behind.

A solid steel door was wide open at the end of the hallway. Flint shoved away the flimsy screen door that was sagging on its hinges and stepped out onto a wooden deck. She swept her arms from side to side, her weapon held up high.

Thornberry followed her outside, guarding the sergeant's back.

The back lot seemed narrower than it was because of the high brick wall that abutted the alley on the right and a tall fence that separated it from the cafe's property on the left. The yard was a jumble of garbage bins and wooden pallets lined against the enclosure. There was barely enough length for a delivery vehicle to fit without its rear end landing up in the lane.

A movement to her left caught Flint's eye. She shouted out but got no answer. From her perch, she could see over the fence to the neighbour next door. A smell of rotting food from the garbage bins wafted over. At the back door, a circle of plastic chairs had faded from sitting outside all year round. Flint couldn't see the appeal of having a break in the midst of the garbage. She thought of looking farther, but figured the shooter was on the run. With one more scan of the yard, she turned around and went back inside, followed closely by Thornberry. They holstered their guns as they walked back to the showroom.

Flint stood over the victim lying lifeless on the floor.

"Is it the owner?" Thornberry asked as she stood beside the sergeant.

"No. It's his assistant. I've seen him in the cafe at lunch time," Flint said. "Could you secure the area before anybody comes by?"

"Sure."

Flint pulled a wallet from the man's back pocket and flipped through the cards. The driver's license had his photo. Stan Kingston. Aged twenty-five.

Thornberry hustled to her vehicle to get the yellow and black tape. She was surprised a crowd hadn't gathered and taken an interest in their activities. Maybe it was because nobody expected anything like this to happen – not here. Even the fireman had departed, probably believing the same.

Flint rubbed her forehead, thinking she had left the violence of the city behind. Her tranquil life in the serene town on the edge of the Pacific Ocean on Vancouver Island, was about to take a turn – for the worse.

Chapter 2

All hell broke loose with the arrival of a black Ford Explorer, sirens blaring and lights flashing. RCMP Constable Gordon Hay pulled the police SUV behind Thornberry's car and squeezed his plus-size frame out from behind the steering wheel. He had been around the block a few times, having served most of his twenty-five years with the police force in the far reaches of the Province of Alberta. It was a desolate, unforgiving landscape with plenty of booze and idle time.

He propped his hat onto his thick gray hair. His duty belt hung low on his ample hips, handcuffs and baton banging against each other as he climbed the steps of the store. RCMP Constable Dennis Jarrett fiddled with his shirt collar before stepping out of the passenger seat, always aware of his appearance – obsessed with how others saw him, especially the women. Although he was nearing the end of his twenties, his dedication to the gym made his short, lean body buff. He wore a short-sleeve shirt to show off his ripped biceps. With a few short strides and a hop up the stairs, he caught up with Hay.

An unmarked hearse drew up, and the pathologist arrived shortly after. Dr. Kelly Churchman, from the BC Coroners Service was a beautiful woman – tall and willowy with the graceful movement of a dancer. She pulled up to the rear of the hearse in her flashy sports car. It didn't matter to her that her parking job was sloppy, she knew it would be a quick in and out. Flint had given her a heads-up on the dire state of affairs.

After that, two more vehicles arrived. A crime scene unit van and the photographer in his personal car. Clad in their white scene-of-crime suits, the team gathered their tools and set to work. The pathologist pushed past everyone without any unnecessary chit-chat and started her examination of the body.

The onlookers on the sidewalk crowded in, pressing against the police tape that had been strung out in a wide arc. They had gathered slowly, one by one, in pairs, and finally in a great sweep of curious people. They were given no information but had to depend on the gossip that was flowing freely now.

The constables stood right inside the doorway so as not to contaminate the crime scene. They huddled together, an unlikely group of individuals, with a murder laid at their feet. Flint gave them a briefing on the situation. It was a shocking moment for Jarrett who had never experienced anything worse than a botched robbery in his duties. He was a home-grown boy.

"The guy is dead," Jarrett said. "Someone shot him. Jesus!"

Flint nodded and addressed Hay. "Okay. There's lots to tackle. I want you and Jarrett to do a quick patrol around the neighbourhood before you go knocking on doors. Maybe the shooter got cold feet and is hiding out somewhere. We wouldn't want to walk right by his lair. Would we?" She looked at the older, wiser constable.

"No, definitely not. We'll take a good look around first. You can count on us." Hay grabbed his partner's shirt and turned to leave.

"Hay."

"Yeah, boss."

"Be careful."

Her furrowed eyebrows told him she was concerned that someone was running around with a gun.

The senior detectives lingered on the stairs as the two constables jumped into their vehicle, switched off the strobing lights and cruised slowly down Main Street. Flint didn't take her eyes off them until they disappeared around a corner, turning north. Even then, she stared straight ahead, a plan formulating in her mind.

The road ran east to west, starting at exit 56, off Highway 1 that ran the full length of the island, and ending at a pristine coastline with secluded beaches and large rollers sweeping in from the other side of the world. Behind the mixture of brick and wood buildings were back lanes for deliveries and garbage trucks on both sides of the street. Beyond that were rows and rows of houses that eventually bumped up against an ancient rainforest, completely shutting them in.

"What about a roadblock? If we're quick enough." Thornberry said, interrupting her sergeant's thoughts. "There's only one way out of this place."

Flint nodded. She too had been thinking this. "Except for the half-dozen logging roads."

"But that's not likely. Is it?"

"But really, we don't know who we're looking for," Flint said.

"Right. I didn't think of that." Thornberry's face flushed a light pink.

Chatter from the crowd floated toward them. The spectators had caught wind of a killer among them.

"Looks like trouble brewing," Flint said. "Do you think you could take control of that, Naomi? Make sure nobody breaches the police tape."

"You bet."

As soon as Thornberry set foot on the pavement someone shouted out at her.

"What's going on in there?" The voice boomed out against the chatter of the crowd.

Flint paused momentarily, then escaped inside.

The corporal slipped on her sunglasses and stood silently by the yellow tape, prepared to keep order.

Footsteps, quick and deliberate, made Thornberry peer over her glasses to a man who was trying to push his way beyond the tape. Beads of sweat dripped from his forehead. His short-sleeved shirt had dark marks under the armpits.

"Whoa! This is a restricted area. Please stand back," Thornberry said. She held out her arm and pressed her hand on his chest to stop his advance.

"What's going on?" The agitated man slapped at her arm. "Let me through."

"No admittance to the public."

"I heard someone tried to rob my store," the man said, his grumpiness shining through. "I need to get in."

"What's your name?" Thornberry asked, although from the description she had been given she realized this was undoubtedly the owner.

"Ben. Ben Altman."

"Okay. Wait here for a sec, sir. I'll get the boss," Thornberry said and climbed up the stairs. She rapped on the door and poked her head into the room, looking around for Flint. She spotted the sergeant talking to the pathologist.

"Hey, Flint. The owner is here."

"Okay, thanks. Tell him I'll be right there."

The corporal shut the door and turned around. The owner had ducked under the tape and stood defiantly by the steps with his arms crossed. Before Thornberry had a chance to say anything, Flint stepped out. She pulled off her blue vinyl gloves and stuck them into a pocket.

"Mr. Altman, I'm Sergeant Flint. I'll be in charge of the investigation." She glanced over the restless throng.

"Where's Stan?" Altman asked and a sudden realization overcame him. "Is he hurt?" The testiness had evaporated from his voice.

"I'm sorry to tell you that your assistant has been shot and killed."

"What? Stan is dead?" Ben almost screamed, then clasped his hand over his mouth. "Oh, my God. What happened?"

"We don't know anything yet. It's still too early to say exactly what occurred here."

Flint didn't want to speak to the owner outside in the open, but she couldn't risk bringing him inside. The evidence had to be protected. So she moved in closer to ask a few questions.

"Was the clerk the only person in the store this morning?"

"No, I popped into the drug store on the corner. I was only gone a short while." Ben shuffled his feet and looked away. "It could have been me that got shot."

Flint didn't comment on that, thinking the man had gotten part of it right. There could have been two bodies.

"Did you notice anything out of the ordinary?"

"Like what?"

"Was there anyone hanging around? Anything like that?"

"No. Nothing. Another regular Monday." Ben rubbed at his mouth.

"Does Stan have family nearby?"

"He told me his parents were dead, but he has a brother in Vancouver. Percy, I think. It's all in my files in the office."

"Okay. We'll get to that. But right now we need the keys to your shop."

"What? Why?"

"It's a crime scene."

Ben screwed up his face about to say something, the prickly demeanour reappearing quickly, but he stopped himself. He dug into his pocket and handed a small ring of assorted keys.

"When can I–"

"We'll let you know when you can have your shop back," Flint interrupted. She was done talking for the time being. There was too much to do. "We'll get a statement from you tomorrow."

"Oh. Okay, I guess." Mr. Ben Altman walked away.

Flint watched him scoot under the police tape and push through the thinning crowd. She went back inside and headed straight for the office. The filing cabinet was butted up against the desk. It had labels on each drawer clearly marking the contents inside. The second one down had only a few folders hanging from side rails. She flicked through them and found the one she was looking for. There were only two sheets in Stan's folder. The first one was a recommendation from a jewelry store in Vancouver. The next one had all the man's personal information, including a contact number in case of an emergency. Flint squared her shoulders and dialled the number.

The man who answered had a husky voice. "Hello."

"Is this Percy Kingston?"

"Yes. Who's this?"

"I'm Sergeant Marlowe Flint from the RCMP in Castlecrest."

"Is this about my brother? Has something happened to him?" A note of fear crept into his voice.

"I'm afraid that I have some bad news. There was an incident this morning and your brother died," Flint said. "Sorry for your loss."

Flint heard a quick intake of breath and a sob. She remained silent to give him a chance to compose himself.

Percy spoke again. "Was it a car accident?"

"No, it happened at his workplace. At the jewelry store. He was shot and killed."

"Shot? He was shot?" Percy asked. "Was it a robbery? Did you arrest the guy?"

"We are at the beginning of our investigations..." Flint started to explain.

"How could this happen? I don't understand. Where does someone even get a gun?" Percy stopped and took a deep breath. "I want to see my brother."

"Of course," Flint said.

"I'll be on the first ferry in the morning."

"Okay. I'll see you–" Flint stopped when she heard the dial tone. Percy had hung up on her.

From behind the counter she heard the pathologist call her name.

"Hang on, Kelly. We'll be right there." Flint peeked out the door and waved Thornberry inside.

The crowd had pretty much left, just a few stragglers with nothing better to do than hang out. The last of them would be in the bar before the streetlights went on, she was sure.

The pathologist stood over the body with her bag clasped in her hand, ready to head off.

"I checked as thoroughly as I could. It looks like the one bullet to his chest. Probably hit his heart. He would have died quickly. There's no exit wound, so I suppose I will have to dig the bullet out."

"Can you give us any more details?"

"Until I do the autopsy tomorrow, that's all I have."

"Thanks, Kelly."

"Come by later in the morning," the pathologist said as she skirted around the body and left.

Flint called the attendants chatting on the bench outside. They grabbed a stretcher and a body bag to take

Stan Kingston away. As she watched them load him up and struggle out the door, an unnerving notion invaded her thoughts. Was there more to come? Another robbery? Another shooting?

Chapter 3

Flint stood in the middle of the room, glancing over the glass cases loaded with expensive looking jewelry and watches. As she raised her face to the cool draft of the overhead fan, she noticed a large black box with a blinking red light tucked in the corner. She couldn't believe her good fortune.

"Aha. Now we've got you."

"What?" Thornberry looked around the room, a bewildered look on her face.

"Take a look at that." Flint pointed to the surveillance camera.

"Holy smokes. Do you think we got the shooter on tape?"

"I sure the hell hope so."

"Cool," Thornberry said.

"The office. Let's go."

The two detectives dashed to the back. Besides the desk and filing cabinet, there was nothing else in the room – no equipment, no recording devices, nothing.

"What the hell!" Flint barked.

"What's wrong?"

"I thought there was a laptop. I'm sure of it."

"Yeah, I saw it. Forensics must have already taken it."

"Of course. Let's go get it," Flint said. She sprinted to the showroom.

Ryan Harper was the only full-time crime scene investigator in their unit. He was working on a section of the glass case nearest to where the victim had fallen. The other two CSIs were busy at the other end of the room. All potential evidence they collected and readied for transport would go to the RCMP crime lab at the Nanaimo station, a harbour city on the east side of the island. The detachment was the major hub for the northern regions of the island with Superintendent Hank Parker as officer in charge of the entire district, including Castlecrest.

Flint stood by the counter as Ryan deftly twirled a fibre brush along the surface, the black dust settling in the grooves of the prints left behind. She knew it would be sheer luck to actually find anything of value, but if anyone could coax some evidence out of the hundreds of fingerprint possibilities, it would be Ryan. Not only did he have fourteen years of field experience, but he was also a forensic scientist with expertise on fingerprints, weapons and firearms. Most scientists only worked in the lab once the evidence was submitted but not Ryan. He worked the crime scene, as well. After he was finished his job here, he would head to the lab two hours drive away and start analysis of the evidence.

Finally, Ryan looked up.

"Did you find a laptop?" Flint asked.

"Yeah. It's been bagged."

"Can we take a look at the video surveillance? Was there a memory stick?"

"The laptop wasn't hooked up to anything," Ryan said. "It wasn't even turned on."

"Oh. That's weird. I must have missed something." Flint went back to the office and pulled the desk away from the wall. There were no cables sticking out of the wall. "Shit."

Thornberry stood by quietly.

"What the hell is going on here?" Flint stormed out of the room.

Thornberry followed her out and watched as Flint grabbed one of the stools lined up in front of the counter and dragged it over to the corner.

Teetering on the padded seat, Flint reached up to the box. The cable came out of the wall with a light tug. She jumped off her perch and landed on the floor with a thud. "Damn, it's fake. Who does that? That's nuts."

"What about the red light?"

"It's run by battery. I have to admit I've seen that before but never with a store full of this kind of merchandise." Flint collapsed on the stool and glanced around the room at the glass cases full of sparkling gems set in gold and platinum. "The owner is a stupid ass."

Thornberry remained silent while Flint ranted for a couple of minutes. It was more like mumbling under her breath. The investigators went about their business unaware of the sergeant's frustration. The sound of metal cases being snapped closed and the shuffling of boxes signalled the men were readying to leave. Behind the counter, Ryan had his gear packed up and was beelining it to the exit. It had been a slow process, but the entire team had systematically worked their way through the crime scene. They had done all they could do.

"Well, I guess that's it for the day," Flint said as the crime scene guys brushed past them in a file. She called out to Ryan before he darted out the door. Another question had popped into her head. "Have you got a moment?"

"Oh, sure. What's up?"

"Were there any shell casings found?"

"No. And no bullets plugged into the wall or ceiling anywhere, either."

"You're sure?"

Ryan narrowed his eyes; his mouth went taut.

"Of course you are. Thanks," Flint said, trying not to wince. The door clicked shut with finality. "Oops. Didn't mean to insult him."

"Oh, he'll get over it," Thornberry said. "Should I lock up the back?"

"Don't bother. Go home. I'll secure the shop," Flint said. "We'll meet up at eight. My office. I'll text Hay and Jarrett."

"Okay. Did you hear from them?"

"Yeah. But they're not crushing it. Not a witness to be found anywhere," Flint said.

"Bummer." Thornberry turned from the doorway, but Flint had already pulled her cell out of her pocket. "See you tomorrow," she whispered and pulled the door shut behind her.

A hush came over the room, the narrow windows in straight rows thwarting any street racket from penetrating through the thick glass. Sleek silver lamps, hung low in sets of twos, had turned on automatically. They threw overly bright beams of light in every direction, not a shadow cast anywhere.

Flint didn't notice any of this as she dialled the superintendent's number. She could feel a tightening in her chest. Not that she feared Hank Parker, but she didn't know him, didn't know what kind of reaction to expect. Although he was support for front line officers, his main job was a liaison between his staff and the public, a very political position. And she had no good news to tell him. She almost hung up, thinking she should wait until she had something, some progress in the investigation to relate. But it was too late.

"Parker here. Speak."

"Hello, Superintendent. It's Sergeant Flint from Castlecrest."

"Hey. We haven't touched bases for quite a while. My fault. Always some conference or meeting."

"Yes, sir. I know you're a busy man–"

"Never mind that," Parker interrupted. "How are things going on the west coast?"

"That's why I'm calling," Flint said.

"Oh, have you got something big in the wind?"

"Yes." Flint gulped.

"Oh, what's going on?"

"There's been a shooting. We have one guy dead in the jewelry store," Flint said. She hesitated before adding, "It could be a robbery, but we don't have many facts as of yet."

"I see," Parker said. "It was bound to happen, sooner or later. You know how that goes. The criminals follow the tourists. You got a shit load of them lately."

"They come by the bus load."

"The word got out about the gigantic rollers on your shoreline. It's quite the thing," Parker said.

"I know." It was a sad thought for Flint. She had grown up in this small town. Nothing worse than a few break-ins and the occasional hold-up had ever happened there. And never with a gun. Not only was their cozy town becoming overrun, but she worried this was the beginning of a crime spree. Coming back home was supposed to be an escape from the craziness of the city.

"Well, not to worry. You were in the homicide department in the Okanagan. Right?"

"Yes, I was stationed in Kelowna for ten years."

"You'll do fine. You have good officers working with you. Hay knows the ropes."

"Hay has a lot of experience," Flint said. She wasn't so sure about Jarrett.

"Call me any time, if you need some extra hands."

Flint looked around the room after the superintendent hung up. She locked up the shop and stepped outside. Darkness had descended upon the day.

Chapter 4

The house was dark except for a lone light shining in the living room. Flint pulled into the driveway and shut off the engine. The two-storey building, clad in white shingles, had hooded dormer windows on the steeply pitched roof that provided good views of the ocean. It had stood on the rocky outcrop since the turn of the last century and had been Flint's childhood home. Although she had moved out after she married, her bedroom had been preserved as if she had never left. Now that she had taken up residence once again, she had stowed the stuffed animals into a box, about to relegate them to the basement, when her young daughter laid claim to them. Paige's room was adjacent to hers, accessible through the Jack and Jill bathroom. It was a perfect setup.

Flint glanced up to the second floor and grit her teeth against the pain that bombarded her during these poignant moments. Martin was dead. He wouldn't see his little girl attend college, get married, have kids. Paige asked about her father less and less as time went on. Soon she would forget him all together. Flint sighed, torn between relief and sorrow. Relief that Paige would carry on, and sad that she wouldn't experience love from her dad in the years ahead. All Flint had thought of after the tragic event was to get them back to the inner circle – to the comfort of her parents. At least her daughter would know that special kind of love from her grandparents. She intended to stay here until Paige was grown up, ready to fly away on her own.

The moon dipped below the horizon as Flint walked up the side of the house to the back entrance. She could hear a low growl before she eased the door open. Bodhi stood up and circled a few times before sitting down in front of her, his golden tail swishing across the wood plank floor. He bared his teeth into a crooked smile, his brown eyes wide in anticipation of an evening romp. Flint rubbed behind his ears.

"Give me a minute."

Bodhi dropped back down on the small rug by the door, resting his head on his paws, his eyes following her as she moved around.

Flint made herself a cup of tea and headed for the living room. Her father sat in his favourite chair with the light shining on his lap, where the book he was reading was closed. A bookmark stuck out from the pages about halfway through the novel. He placed his hand on the cover and tapped the leather.

"It doesn't get much better than this. *The Spy Who Loved Me*. One of Ian Fleming's best stories. Although, it was poorly received at first." Victor Sullivan rubbed the cover and smiled. "Not anymore. I was lucky to get this."

Flint knew it was a first edition, first print book. Her dad was a serious collector of rare books. She sat on the edge of the couch, feeling drained. But the sound of his voice was like a fluffy towel after a dip in the cold ocean, so she closed her eyes and let him ramble.

"I have another James Bond novel. *Moonraker*. It's a first edition, but second printing." He continued with his musings. "Not as valuable as this one." He placed it on the table beside his armchair and looked over to his girl, all grown up.

"You look tired, honey."

"It was a really long day," Flint said with a sigh.

"I heard."

"I bet. Gossip spreads like wildfires around here."

"Dale called..."

"Oh, crap. I forgot we were going out for drinks at the pub," Flint said. "There's a new band playing tonight."

"Not to worry. He knew you were caught up in the incident down at the jewelry store."

"It's a homicide, dad."

"I thought so."

Flint pulled her cell out, then looked at her watch. It was too late to phone now.

"Did Dale say anything else?"

"Yes, as a matter of fact he did." Victor narrowed his eyes and stared at her.

"What?"

"He wanted to know what Paige's favourite colour was."

"Oh."

"Are you and the fire chief getting serious?"

"No, not at all." Dale Begley wasn't Martin, and besides Flint didn't want to get too close to anybody. Not yet anyway. It was too soon.

"So, what's going on?" Victor asked.

Flint knew her father was only concerned with her welfare. He wasn't trying to pry into her affairs. She loved him for that.

"Dale wanted to get something for Paige's birthday. I guess he wanted to make sure it would be the right colour. You know how fussy kids are."

"I do. You hated the colour purple," Victor said.

"I don't remember that."

"Well I do, dear," her mom piped up. Oleane stood in the doorway, her green housecoat pulled together at the neck with both hands. "Your aunt and uncle bought you a beautiful outfit for Christmas one year. You tossed it to the ground after seeing the purple trim along the bottom of the dress." She shook her head and smiled at the memory. "You never did wear it. What a shame."

Flint rose to her feet. "Did I wake you, Mom?"

"No. I came down to see if my husband was ever coming to bed."

"I'm coming now." Victor stretched out his back before standing up. "See you in the morning, Marlowe." He squeezed her shoulder before turning away.

"What did you tell him?" Flint asked.

"Who?"

"Dale. About the colour."

"Blue, of course," her dad replied and walked down the hallway after his wife.

Flint laughed. Her little girl was crazy about the colour. Blue bike, blue clothes. Newly painted bedroom in a shade of blue. Thank goodness she was still too young to dye her hair.

Flint tip-toed up the stairs. She paused on the landing to listen for any sound from Paige's room. Nothing. After sneaking a quick peek at her daughter snuggled up with her favourite teddy bear, Flint moved down the hallway to her own room. She stowed her gun into its safe, put her badge on the counter, grabbed a small packet that was hidden in her socks drawer and headed back downstairs. A soft thumping from the kitchen told Flint that Bodhi had heard her creeping around the house. The dog rose when she entered the room.

"Good boy, let's go." Flint picked up the flashlight from the shelf in the mudroom in case it got dark before they headed back.

As soon as they hit the trail, Flint lit up a cigarette. She drew in a deep breath and let it out slowly. One cigarette at the end of each day. That's what she allowed herself to get over her husband's death. Flint sucked in another lungful and blew it out.

"Don't worry, pal. I'll stop this soon."

Bodhi glanced up, then stuck his nose back to the path. He moved forward only a few metres before circling back to Flint and starting the routine again. After they reached the first set of stairs leading down to the water, Flint stopped.

"Is that enough? Or do you want to run on the beach?"

Bodhi's ears pricked up, tilting his head at the question. Then he disappeared, game on. The old rustic stairs shuddered as Flint bounded after him. The retriever ran the length of the beach and back, kicking up the sand as he galloped past her. His long fur soaked up the water as he jumped in and out of the waves. At the last turn, he stood in front of Flint and gave his body a mighty shake, dousing her from head to toe. He sat down by her feet as if nothing untoward had happened, his lip curling into a smile.

"Thanks for that." Flint swiped her hand across her mouth. "Time to go." As they made their way back along the path, the last of the sun's rays faded. She turned on the flashlight and quickened her pace.

After drying off the dog, Flint left her sandy shoes at the kitchen door and made her way through the darkened house. She flipped on her bedroom light and closed the door. As usual, she was drawn to the window. She sat on the cushion in the small niche and tilted the sash to let in the warm air. The wind had picked up in the last hour, so she could hear the crashing of the surf on the rocks below. She stared out to an infinite blackness. White frothy caps tumbling over each other were barely visible. She tossed her clothes on a nearby chair and slipped on a pink nightgown, the last present from Martin. Flint ran her hand along the silky fabric, thinking back to his touch.

After brushing her teeth and switching off the last light, she lay still on the bed. The totality of darkness frightened her. She tried breathing in and out with purpose, but the fear was so powerful she felt her heart flutter against her chest. Her throat closed in as she tried to swallow. It wasn't the darkness itself that was frightening, but the fear of what that darkness might hide that paralyzed her. Beads of sweat had gathered on her temple. She brushed away the dampness and sat up. She wasn't sure she would ever escape her fear, not after what happened to Martin. It left her feeling vulnerable and exposed. Flint jumped out of bed and switched on the bathroom light. She pulled the door so that a narrow beam of light cut through the blackness, then leaned back against the pillow. Her body shook ever so slightly as she drifted off to sleep, into her daily nightmare.

The day had dawned crisp and clear, the sun slowly creeping over the snowy mountains. As plans were being finalized, an icy fog blanketed the valley. There was a moment when the police inspector contemplated postponing the raid. He had stared out the window at the mottled sky and had decided there was no chance of a snowfall. This was their window of opportunity. It was a risky undertaking, but the team had prepared well.

Dressed like SWAT officers, the special eight-man squad surrounded the drug house and waited in the bitter cold. The evening sun cast long shadows on the ground as the clouds moved into an almost unbroken layer and extinguished the last rays. Still the inspector radioed for all officers to hold position. As Flint waited, her back against the wall, she heard the occasional barking of faraway dogs that broke the silence of the night. She knew the inspector wouldn't proceed until absolute darkness descended upon them, making them ghostly figures among the pattern of nightly shadows.

In those chilled minutes, she watched the roadway carefully.

Then. Boom. Boom. Boom.

The suspect had bolted out the front door.

A shout. Men running like hell down the street, boots on the ground pounding, the crunch of dry snow sounding above the racket. Toward the alley.

Flint followed, gun in hand, equipment slapping her thighs. Quickly. Trying to steady herself on the slick surface. Her senses heightened. Her fear barely held at bay. She reached the alley, her hands cold and numb. Just a few steps into the alley, and she froze.

Flint started to breath rapidly, wanting to turn and flee. Muffled voices assaulted her ears as she stood wavering on the spot. The pounding in her head almost drowned out the report of the next round of gunshots that reverberated between the brick walls. Finally, she found the nerve to enter the alley. She stumbled to the man on the ground, blood oozing from his body. The inspector. Martin. Her husband.

Flint awoke with a start at five in the morning, an uneasy feeling lingering. She dragged herself out of bed and headed to the shower. It was a new day, but would it be a new night? Or the same fear gripping her heart?

Chapter 5

The newly built RCMP detachment was on a side street behind the movie theatre on the north side of town. It was a plain, squat building with few distinct attributes, except for the gorgeous ocean views from every room at the back. Flint's team occupied the north end with their own entry. The main entrance on the south end made up the rest of the detachment with four constables, one of whom was a community constable, and the office staff.

Oblivious to the passing of time, Flint had her head bent down, feverishly working on the incident report. The clock above the bookcase made a dull sound as the minute hand swept past the top of the hour. She glanced up from her computer screen and stared out of the window, rubbing at her bloodshot eyes with the back of her hand. The rising sun cast a pearly hue across the morning sky, promising another hot day. The brightening light reflected off the black glass surface of her desk. A desk void of any bric-a-brac, only a single framed photo of her little girl on a swing.

Flint leaned back in her leather chair and ran her eyes around the workspace. Overstuffed chairs scattered about and a large sectional sofa bordering two walls were dwarfed by the immense size of the room. Three filing cabinets within easy reach stood to her right. Colourful rugs covered most of the hideous grey vinyl floor and managed to pull the space together into a welcoming office. She felt comfortable here.

With renewed energy, Flint skimmed her fingers across the keyboard and deftly typed in another paragraph. This was the beginning of the case file. The murder book. It would be a complete paper trail of the murder investigation, starting from the time the murder was first reported. Follow-up reports would be added daily from each person involved. Crime scene photographs, autopsy and forensic reports, witness interviews, sketches, and notes would all find their way into the book. How thick it became depended on a lot of factors. Even if the case wasn't solved, the uniform structure of the book allowed anyone involved in the homicide investigation to review and locate key reports. It could even land up in the cold case files. That was not a thought Flint wanted to entertain. She saved her work to the digital file that would go to headquarters, printed out her report and placed it in the book. She closed the lid of her laptop as the clock clunked another hour gone by and the first constable arrived.

"Sergeant." Jarrett tapped on the door frame.

"Have a seat." Flint waved him in.

The constable sank into a deep-cushioned armchair. He struggled to plant his boots on the ground, so he pushed himself up to perch on the edge of his seat.

"Good morning, Sergeant," Constable Hay said. He sat down heavily on the sofa, seemed almost to collapse into it.

Corporal Thornberry's weighty footfalls echoed down the hallway before she appeared, out of breath. As usual. Her rosy cheeks with small dimples glowed, and her hair fell in ringlets about her perfect skin.

Flint's team seemed as knackered as she felt. Yesterday had been excruciating for everyone. They had been flung out of their comfort zone. She looked at each member in turn, wondering who would hold up and who would flounder during the investigation. Jarrett was the only person she had real concern for. He was young and inexperienced in this type of case.

"First and foremost, we need to get our reports written up each and every day. Every detail. Right?" Flint said.

Nobody spoke, but they all nodded in agreement. Jarrett's feet were bouncing on the floor.

"We'll set up in the boardroom."

Without any fanfare, Flint stood up. At the end of the hallway, she unlocked the last door on the left and entered. The team filed in behind her.

The room was bare bones, outfitted with a long table and a dozen office chairs. A built-in cabinet at the end of the room had a white laminate countertop with a coffee maker and toaster at the ready. No fancy granite or leather, only functional furniture. Although, as if to make up for the minimalistic decor, the view from here was twice as dynamic as that from her office. More notably impressive than the rise and fall of the colossal waves was a stone structure that seemed out of place in the dense rain forest. For beyond the boundary of the municipality stood a castle on a point of land that reached out into the unforgiving sea. Not really a castle, but a mansion built by the founder of the town, Charles Crest. Its long ago past shrouded in mystery, forgotten by all except by a few old-timers. The dwelling was now a destination hotel for all the tourists who invaded their placidity.

After everyone sat in their usual spots, Flint waited until she had their full attention before she began.

"We have been trained for this course of events," Flint said. "It is no different than any other investigation we have all done countless times." She held up her hand as Jarrett was about to interrupt. "The only difference is the seriousness of the crime." She paused. "And quite possibly, there is an element of danger to all of us. Our team. And the public. With a killer on the loose who is in possession of a gun. Unless it has been tossed. So be mindful at all times. Okay?"

The impression of peril that had sprouted in her mind yesterday had taken root. Flint didn't want to instil panic, but she couldn't shake the feeling loose. Hopefully, what she said came across as a sort of pep talk with a warning. Although truthfully, they all knew murder was a game changer. She looked at the faces of her teammates to see the reaction. Thornberry looked up to the challenge, almost enthusiastic. Flint figured she was a good team member. Hay nodded emphatically, lips pressed together in determination, having been involved in more deaths than anyone on the team. Jarrett looked scared. She would have to help the constable find some inner strength to get through each day. It was going to be rough for him otherwise.

To get things moving along, Flint stood up and walked over to the incident board that was set up against the far wall. The stark white surface would soon be covered with varying lines of colour, scribbling and pictures taped along the border.

Flint picked up a black marker and sketched a circle with lines radiating out like the spokes of a wheel. At these points, she drew large boxes. She labelled the centre one with 'Victim' in a red crayon and wrote in 'Stan Kingston'.

"We'll start here." She turned to her audience. "Why him? What do we know about him?" Her team drew blank faces.

"He's from Vancouver. Worked in a jewelry store there before coming here." She turned back to the board and started writing. "He's twenty-five years old. His only family is a brother who still lives in Vancouver. That's it. Not much."

"Was it a random robbery then, do you think?" Jarrett asked.

"Could be. But we can't assume anything yet. We don't know what's missing yet, if anything."

Flint thought it might be easier to go with a random shooting. Wipe their hands clean and be done with it. The chaos that could ensue if the killer was someone the victim knew wasn't worth thinking about.

"What about witnesses? Any luck with that?" Flint asked.

"No. We did a cruise around the neighbourhood first. Then we parked by the fire hall on the corner and worked our way up the street," Hay said. "We went into every store, but nobody saw a thing."

"The window-shoppers will be long gone," Flint said. "But someone might step up once the word gets out about the shooting."

"We also checked out the houses that back onto the lane behind the store. Zilch," Jarrett added.

"Nobody heard the shot, either?" Flint asked.

"No," Jarrett said.

Flint doubted most people would have even realized it was a gunshot. Not in this laid-back town. Not the surfers and their entourage that claimed the breakers, not the tourists that roamed the town taking selfies with the giant trees, and certainly not the locals who ignored everything.

"What about the people in the Seabreeze Cafe? That's where I was when I heard the shot," Flint said.

"The coffee shop wasn't open by the time we got there. I guess they closed up early," Jarrett said.

"Not a big surprise. Thornberry and I will go there later and sort that out."

"By the way, the bank was closed, too," Hay said.

"Okay. We'll go there, as well." Flint picked up a marker and labelled the boxes: Suspects? DNA? Fingerprints? Weapon? She turned back to the team. "All we have to do is fill in the blanks."

"Sure, boss." Hay laughed.

"I want you and Jarrett to pick up the shop owner and bring him into the station. He's expecting you. We need to get a statement from him."

"No problem."

"And after you get back, head over to the store." Flint tossed him a large set of keys. "You know that part where we don't know what's missing. Well, you have the privilege of doing the inventory. Lots of loose diamonds landed up on the floor."

Hay groaned. Jarrett looked relieved.

Chapter 6

"Give me back my..." The raised voice waned into an indiscernible babble.

Flint was seated at her desk and looked up at the commotion coming from the front of the building. Thornberry, sitting in a chair across from her, stifled a laugh.

"You can't do this to me. I'm putting in a complaint. What's your badge number?" The words became louder and clearer as the person strode down the passageway toward the sergeant's office. Then the approaching footsteps stopped quick as lightning, and there was a sharp rap on the door.

"Come in," Flint said, leaning back into her chair.

Constable Jarrett stuck his head around the corner. "We have Mr. Altman."

A pudgy, hook-nosed man barged into the room.

"I thought I was coming here to get my keys back, not get the third degree."

Flint waited until he had had his say. "Thank you, Constable." She smiled at Jarrett who backed out from the doorway. "Have a seat, Mr. Altman."

Ben glared at the detectives and plunked himself into a chair.

"We're sorry for the inconvenience this–" Flint paused "–event has caused you. We are doing our best to get it sorted out quickly, so you can re-open your store."

"I should think so. That officer was rude to me," Ben said.

"I'll have a talk with him. Don't you worry." Flint cast a sideways glance at Thornberry and rolled her eyes.

"Fine." Ben crossed his arms.

"Your store is still a crime scene, Mr. Altman. We should be done soon."

"Today?" Ben scowled.

"No, but soon. We're doing our best. Remember we have a killer to find."

"I suppose. Poor Stan." A smidgen of guilt made his face blush. He sat back. "So, why am I here?"

"We need to get a statement from you," Flint said.

"What kind of statement? I wasn't there when... you know, it happened."

"We need some background info. Could you tell me how long Stan worked for you?" Flint often asked questions that she knew the answer to, merely to see how frank a person was.

"Six months. Business has been good. I needed some help," Ben said.

"Stan came from Vancouver," Flint said. She stopped to look at her notes. "From a store on Granville. The Goldsmith Bros. Is that correct?"

"Yes. I spoke to Mr. Smith personally. He gave Stan a good recommendation. Hard worker. Always on time." Ben smiled.

"Has it worked out that way? Was Stan living up to his reputation?" Flint wished she had worded that differently, now that the man was dead.

"Yes. And we got along, as well."

"Good. Now I want to ask about the surveillance camera."

"What about it?" Ben asked, a bit more belligerent than he needed to be.

"Was there a reason for the phony setup?"

"Look, I'm the victim here," he said and glared at the sergeant.

Flint didn't respond. She glanced at Thornberry who sat coolheaded, taking it all in.

Mr. Altman grew quiet, his eyes down on the desk in front of him. "I couldn't afford a proper security system."

"I thought you said business was going well." Flint lowered her gaze to the paper on her desk and tapped it with her pen.

"Cameras are expensive," Ben blustered. "So what?"

"Is there anything else you would like to tell me?" She looked up at him.

"No." Ben drew in a breath and whispered, "You won't say anything to my insurance company?"

"Not our concern," Flint said flatly. "Is the inventory list in your ledger accurate, Mr. Altman?"

"What do you need that for?" He pursed his lips.

"It's all part of the investigation. To see if anything was stolen during the shooting. We need to be certain. So, is it?"

"Yes."

"That will do for now. Thank you for your cooperation in this matter. We'll be in touch if we need anything else."

Mr. Altman pushed his chair back from the desk and left without a word.

Flint looked up at the clock. "I have time to make a quick call to Mr. Smith before we head over to the morgue."

"Sure."

Flint dialled the store in Vancouver and spoke to the owner for several minutes before hanging up.

"He confirms everything that Mr. Altman said."

Thornberry nodded.

"He was shaken up about Stan's death," Flint said. "Said Stan had a hard time a while ago, but pulled out of it."

"About his parents dying?"

"That's what he thought. Anyway, he liked Stan. He was sorry to see him go when he did."

"Makes you wonder sometimes."

"About what?"

"About the choices you make. Stan leaves the big city where there's lots of crime, and then look what happens. You know, like it was meant to be," Thornberry said.

"Yeah, I do know." Flint had those thoughts running through her head on a never-ending loop. If only. She started the engine and headed to the hospital.

* * *

The Hotel Dieu Hospital was on Woodruff Street on the outskirts of town. The red brick building stood back from the road about thirty metres. Flint cruised along the tree-lined drive that cut through a grassy meadow and ended in a large parking lot. The morgue was at the back on the lower floor of the three-storey structure. She pulled into a spot, beside a flashy sportscar, under a large maple tree that shaded a portion of the stalls reserved for official vehicles.

As they walked along the sidewalk, the sweet fragrance of a butterfly bush wafted through the air. The large purple flowers nodded at the ends of their blue-green foliage. Thornberry took a deep breath. "How lovely."

"Hold that thought," Flint said. She laughed. "Or maybe I should say, hold that breath."

"Funny."

They walked down the hallway, passing a number of offices, before they got to the morgue. Thornberry rapped on the door and swung it open. They were hit with a flow of stagnant air mixed with a combination of chemicals that put a taste of metal in their mouths. Adding to the tang, the washed-out tones of the grey walls had a lingering smell of bleach. Everything was clean, sterile. But the stench put Thornberry on edge.

Dr. Kelly Churchman looked up at the sound of the intruders.

"Oh, good. You're right on time." The pathologist pulled back a white sheet that covered the victim's body. "There are no surprises. He died from a gunshot wound, a single bullet. It hit his heart and killed him instantly. Bad luck really."

She pointed to a simple hole in his chest.

The two detectives leaned in to get a good look. It looked so innocuous.

"That's it?" Thornberry asked.

"There are no marks on his hands or forearms. No defence wounds of any kind."

"So it appears as if the killer walked right into the store and shot our guy," Flint said. "Probably thought he was a customer."

"Or he knew the person," Thornberry said.

"That's for you to determine," Churchman replied. She pulled the sheet back over the body and marched over to a counter along the far wall. "Here's your bullet. A bit of fragmentation, but all in all, not bad." She passed a bag marked 'evidence' to the sergeant. "I've seen way worse."

"Will you send it right over to the lab?" Flint asked as she examined the bullet.

"Without question," Churchman said. "Ryan's a toolmark expert. He should be able to match this up with the murder weapon."

"Ryan could, if we had the murder weapon," Flint said.

"Well, good luck with that," Churchman said. "Sorry I couldn't be of much help. I can confirm the time of death, but you were there so that's a moot point. Is someone coming to identify the body?"

"Yes." Flint's cell rang. She glanced at the screen. "That's him now. Hang on." She made her way outside, skirted along the side of the building to the front. A tall, handsome man stood by the entrance. He was almost a replica of the person lying on the metal table inside.

Flint pulled out her badge as she approached the man.

"Hello. I'm Sergeant Flint." She held out her hand.

"Percy Kingston." His grip was firm and dry.

"Yes. Are you ready?"

He lowered his head slightly and drew in a deep breath. "Okay."

"Just along here," Flint said as they made their way to the morgue.

Percy walked with long, decisive steps. Although Flint had long legs, she had to pick up speed to keep pace with him. They headed inside and walked down the wide hallway. She stopped in front of an open door and gestured him inside.

The pathologist sat at a table with an envelope in front of her. Thornberry sat beside her. There was a couch positioned along one wall with a picture of a valley meadow at sunrise above it. It was a plain but comfortable space for viewing.

"Have a seat," Flint said and pulled a chair out.

"Okay."

"You'll be fine. We're here to help you," Churchman said.

Percy looked around at the others and drew his lips into a white line.

Churchman took the photograph out of the envelope and placed it face down. "We have identified the victim as your brother. This is just to make it official. Take your time." She flipped the paper over and slid it across the table.

Percy looked at the photo, his breathing slow and steady. "That's him. That's Stan." He placed his hands on the tabletop and closed his eyes for a moment.

"I'm sorry for your loss," Flint said.

"Shouldn't I see the body?"

"That's not necessary."

"I suppose not. It won't bring him back," Percy said.

"Would you like us to arrange for some grief counseling?" Churchman asked.

"No, I'll manage."

"We'll find who did this," Flint said.

"I want to take Stan home. To Vancouver. So, I can bury him with our parents." His pleading eyes made Flint swallow hard.

"Of course," Churchman said. "Would you like to go for a coffee before you head back?"

"No, I'm good. I'll just head back home," Percy said. He stood up.

"I'll show you out," Flint said.

Flint walked him to the front of the building.

"Thanks," Percy said.

"I'll let you know when we can release the body."

Percy nodded and turned away.

Flint watched his retreating figure.

"Shit. I shouldn't have given him my word," she muttered to herself. Although she had solved tons of homicide cases before, she had never been the person in charge. She knew she had made a big mistake making promises. Would it be the first of many?

Chapter 7

"This is bullshit," Hay said. "How much stuff does this guy have?"

Jarrett kept his head down and smiled. Doing the inventory was fine with him. A murder investigation was way beyond anything he expected he would ever have to deal with. There was a part of him that worried he would mess up somehow. He studied the different coloured stones, not knowing a ruby from an emerald. He was quite sure a sapphire was blue. But in the end, it didn't matter that he had no knowledge of these precious jewels. All he had to do was find the corresponding stock number in the catalogue and mark the box with a Sharpie pen. He sighed softly.

"We're going to be here all week," Hay said gruffly, wanting a little bit more action.

Jarrett ignored him and pulled a tray out of the glass case, placing it on the counter. The first ring he picked up had three red stones in a gold setting. He held it up to the light. It glistened like fresh drawn blood. He wiped the sweat from his forehead, trying not to think of that. With a deftness of touch, he drew his finger down the page until he found the item. He checked it off and moved on to the next piece. It was a slow, methodical process that suited him well.

"More like two weeks," Hay mumbled from the other end of the counter as he yanked another tray out.

* * *

Flint turned up the radio as she drove them into town. She needed to think without interruption, and her corporal tended to ramble.

Thornberry got the hint. She opened her window all the way, sucking in the clean air. Getting the stench from the morgue out of her nostrils was her top priority. She didn't want to talk anyway.

"I could use a bite to eat while we're here. What do you say?" Flint parked in the lane behind the Seabreeze Cafe.

"I guess," Thornberry said, the queasiness not quite gone. She looked at the Ford Explorer next door. "I wonder how the boys are doing with the inventory?"

"It's a thankless job, but we need to know if anything was stolen," Flint said. "It could change the direction of our investigation."

"Have we got a direction?" Thornberry asked.

All the corporal got in reply was a dirty look, mostly because Flint didn't have an answer for that. She couldn't decide if this case was personal or a random act of violence. Neither one was appealing. But it was only the second day. Still lots of questions to ask before the path to the truth was revealed.

Flint hopped out of the vehicle and strolled down the lane.

"Where are you going?" Thornberry asked as she tried to catch up with Flint.

"The bank first. Wouldn't want to miss them the second time around."

"Definitely not."

They walked toward the narrow alley that separated the bank and the jewelry store. For Flint, it was aptly named Shark Alley. She looked around fearfully and shivered slightly as she entered, the cool darkness descending ominously upon her. If she spread her arms out, she would almost be able to touch both buildings. The walls towered two stories over their heads, blocking out most of the sunlight.

Flint hurried along the passageway to the exit and let out a deep breath once she felt the sunlight on her face.

Thornberry looked up at the surveillance camera bolted under the eaves of the bank building. Its round red globe was the size of a basketball.

"Their security looks pretty skookum."

"Let's hope it captured something useful," Flint said as she opened the door to the bank.

The detectives nodded at the security guard at the front entrance and strolled up to the receptionist desk. A middle-aged lady with dark hair and olive skin smiled at their approach.

"How may I help you, Sergeant?"

"Hi, Tanya. Is Mrs. Shaver free?" Flint asked.

"Let me check," the receptionist said. She punched in a number on her pad to dial the manager. After a short exchange of words, she hung up. "Go ahead. You know the way."

"Thanks."

They walked down a hallway on the right and stopped at the first door. Flint knocked lightly and peeked inside.

"Come on in. Take a load off your feet," Mrs. Shaver said, gesturing to the two chairs in front of her desk. "I heard the news. Is it true? Someone was killed?"

"Yes, the store clerk."

"Holy smokes! Is there something I can do for you?"

"A couple of things, actually," Flint said as she settled into the comfy chair.

"Anything at all that we can help with. You only have to ask."

"The security camera outside. I'm assuming it works."

"Yes, of course." Mrs. Shaver smiled and glanced at both detectives.

"Excellent. Would it be too much to hope that it has more than a day's loop on it?"

"Yes, it does, as a matter of fact. It records a full week before it gets overwritten."

"Perfect." Flint rubbed her hands together, feeling some forward movement in the case.

"I'll get someone to put that together for you straight away. What was the second thing?"

"We would like to talk to everyone that was working yesterday," Flint said.

"I see. I wasn't here myself. Let me find out who was," Mrs. Shaver said and got up. "One moment."

The detectives could hear her speaking to someone in the hallway. Then moments later, she returned.

"We're in luck. Everyone who worked yesterday is here."

"Could we use your office for the interviews?" Flint asked. "If it's not too much to ask."

"No problem. Should I send them in one at a time?"

"We would appreciate that."

Mrs. Shaver shuffled some papers on her desk to the side. "There you go."

"Thank you for your co-operation," Flint said.

After Mrs. Shaver left, Flint switched places and sat in the manager's chair. Thornberry grabbed a seat by a filing cabinet along the far wall. A few moments later, a young girl dressed smartly in a tan and black suit stood in the doorway.

"Come in," Flint said and gestured to a chair. "We have a few questions. It won't take up a lot of your time."

The sergeant pursued her line of questioning in an orderly fashion while Thornberry took notes. As each employee was grilled, Flint's frustration grew. Nobody heard the gunshot. Nobody saw any unusual activity yesterday or the days before.

"How is that even possible?" Flint asked when they were alone.

Thornberry shrugged.

After the last person left, Mrs. Shaver returned and stood in the doorway.

"Were we any help?"

"It all helps," Flint said, although she was thinking it was a bust like everywhere else.

"We'll have the video ready for you tomorrow. Is that all right?"

"Absolutely. Appreciate it," Flint said. She was glad the manager didn't fuss about her getting a warrant for it.

The detectives nodded to the security guard as they left the building.

"Surely, it wasn't only me and the fireman who heard the shot?" Flint stopped in her tracks. "That reminds me. I need to speak to Teddy."

"I'm sitting," Thornberry said, and sat down on the bench in front of Altman's.

"Let's call Teddy and meet him over at the cafe," Flint said.

"Okay, sounds good," Thornberry said.

* * *

The detectives entered the coffee shop and sat at the counter on the only two empty stools left. Giggles and boisterous laughter from the back made Flint swing around and take a look. Standing in front of the last booth crowded with the usual teenagers was the missing waitress, a small order pad in her hand.

"Coffee, ladies? Freshly brewed," Paula asked. The owner placed two mugs in front of them without waiting for a reply.

"Glad to see you got your waitress back," Flint said. She was relieved that no one had filed a missing person's report. The unit had enough on their plate without looking for young people who wandered around aimlessly and not telling anybody.

"What's her story?"

"Oh, Lorie. She said she left me a message on the answering machine. Said she was sick. I didn't see the message," Paula said. Her lips puckered for a moment before breaking into a mirthless smile. "I'm desperate. Of course, I let her come back to work. What can you do?"

Flint glanced at the waitress. For a brief moment, they locked eyes.

"Did you hear the shot, yesterday I mean?" Flint asked as she turned her attention back to the counter.

"No, to be honest, I didn't. Something got your ass moving quickly, but I was too busy to notice anything, being shorthanded and all." Paula said the last bit in a raised voice. Before she even had time to roll her eyes, Lorie came up to them with a chirpy smile.

"Hi." The waitress tore off the piece of paper with the new order on it and slapped it on the shelf of the kitchen hatch. Then she scurried away without a second look in their direction.

"Do you know the victim, Paula? Stan Kingston. The clerk at the jewelry store," Flint said, keenly watching the fleeing waitress.

"He came in for lunch almost every day. Nice guy."

"Did you ever see him sitting with anyone? Or talking to anyone?"

Paula screwed up her face before answering.

"Not really. Maybe Lorie. He seemed like a loner. Sorry, I don't know anything about him."

"That's okay. But I'll want to speak to all the staff that were here."

"Use my office. It's across from the employee lunchroom," Paula said. She swung around at the ding of a bell and came back with burgers and fries. "On the house. I'm pretty sure you guys haven't eaten."

"Awesome. Thanks," Thornberry said, squirting ketchup on her plate.

The bell dinged again. Paula grabbed two steaming plates and headed toward a couple holding hands across the table.

"I think I'll have a chat with Lorie, as well. Even though she wasn't here," Flint said to no one in particular as she munched on her burger.

Thornberry chewed on a pickle, not paying any attention to anything except her plate.

The door made a loud bang as it hit the frame. Teddy, in a pair of shorts and a loose tee shirt, paused at the doorway. After looking around, the fireman headed toward the detectives and plopped his elbows on the edge of the countertop. He leaned forward with a wide smile.

"Hey."

"Thanks for coming," Flint said. She knew him fairly well and liked him. Everyone at the fire hall was community-minded, but Teddy was especially selfless in a way that was harder and harder to find in a person.

Thornberry gaped at the muscles that bulged on his arms.

"I was having a workout. We have a gym tucked in behind the firetrucks." He tugged at his sweaty tee shirt. "Sorry."

The corporal dropped her head to her chin when he looked her way, not meaning to stare.

"I'll be short. What were you doing at the jewelry store?" Flint asked.

"Yesterday? Passing by. I was off-duty and headed for the Seabreeze when I heard the shot. It was loud. I knew it for what it was, and I knew it came from Altman's. Before I could do anything, there you were." Teddy paused. "The rumour is the store clerk was killed."

"That's right. Stan Kingston."

"Oh, shit. That's lousy."

"Where did you go after?"

"I'm not a suspect, am I?" Teddy asked in a good-natured teasing manner.

"No. Of course not," Flint said. "I'm working out the timeline of everyone."

"I hung around for a while to see if I could be of assistance. But you had it under control, so I went to the cafe."

"Wasn't it closed?"

"Yeah, it was. So I went back to the fire hall," Teddy said. "I wasn't sure what to do. Going home didn't seem right. I talked to the guys about what happened. Everyone was freaked out. You know. A shooting right here, in town. We didn't know if anyone was hurt or not. Not then."

"You didn't see anybody running or anything suspicious?"

"No."

Thornberry stopped scribbling in her notebook and looked up.

"That's all we need. Thanks for your time, Teddy. If we have any more questions, we'll get in touch."

"Sure. I guess, I better get back to work." He tapped the countertop and left, glancing back at Thornberry with great curiosity.

The corporal closed her pad and placed it in a pocket, keeping her head down.

"Hay and Jarrett went to the fire hall already. Right?" Flint asked.

"Yeah. The crew there is pretty tight. They hang out with their own. Nobody really knew Stan except to see him on the street or in the bar," Thornberry said. She gathered her long, loose hair and tied it into a ponytail with a bungee. "Teddy's nice," she added, looking outside as the fireman passed by the large front window.

Flint perceived a shift in the shadows. In one fluid movement, she swivelled around on her stool and caught Lorie staring at her. Lorie's cheeks blushed the same red as her hair.

What the hell is her problem? Flint thought.

Chapter 8

"Let's get started with the kitchen staff." Flint turned to her corporal who nodded in agreement.

When she glanced back, Lorie had disappeared.

The detectives walked past the booths at the back. Halfway down the corridor, an insistent stream of conversation rose above the noisy clattering of pots and pans. Flint took a look through a tiny oval window, then pushed on the swinging door. The sound of chatter came to a standstill.

The spotless kitchen was fitted with the latest models of ranges and refrigerators, all shiny stainless steel. Utensils on hooks hung over a long, sleek worktop in the centre of the room. Flint was surprised at the contrast between the modernised facilities and the way Paula ran her cafe. Old-fashioned values intertwined with the latest smart appliances.

Rick, the kitchen hand, poised with a large knife in his hand looked up at them. After a friendly nod, he went back to his task, landing a sharp blow on the scored chopping block. A kid, with a spotty complexion and tousled brown hair held in place with a net, peeled potatoes next to him. A grumpy expression made Flint think he was well-suited for behind the scene work. He pushed at his bangs every few minutes, unable to hide his discomfort. The sizzle of the deep-fryer was louder than the radio playing softly on a shelf above a stack of plates. The cook scooped several pieces of battered fish out of the hot oil before spinning around.

"Hey. You can't be in here." He wiped his forehead with the back of his hand.

"You must be Kyle Ingram," Flint said.

"Yeah. What of it?" A mischievous smile played on his lips, showing a fondness for causing trouble.

"I'm Sergeant Flint. This is Corporal Thornberry. We're investigating the shooting next door and would like to speak to everyone."

Her pleasant tone betrayed what she really wanted to do, which was to give him a good dressing-down. His rough and tumble attitude displayed itself so clearly. But she had experience getting around miscreants way worse than this guy.

The kid looked up, his crystal blue eyes widening. Flint picked him to interview first. Let Kyle think he had won the first round with his flippant words.

They made their way down to Paula's office. It was more the size of a closet. There was a small desk and chair with two more chairs along the wall. No windows. Even with the light switched on, it was dingy.

"Have a seat, Tim," Flint said. She sat down and gestured to the boy.

Thornberry stood in the doorway.

"I didn't see anything," Tim blurted out before the sergeant could say anything.

"I realize that, but did you hear the gunshot?" Flint shifted her eyes to the kid, her gaze steady as she assessed his nervous manner.

"I heard there was only one shot," Tim said.

"So, you didn't hear it yourself?" Flint repeated.

"No."

"Do you know the victim? Stan Kingston, the clerk at the jewelry store?"

"I've seen him in here. Lots. But I don't know anything about him." Tim shrugged, his bony shoulders almost touching his ears.

"Did he talk to anyone? Or–"

"No."

Flint studied the kid for a moment. "All right, that's good. If you think of anything, give us a call." She held out a glossy black card.

Tim took it reluctantly and flipped it over. "Whoa! Nice." He gushed over the gold embossed print before sticking it into his apron pocket. "Okay. See you around." He jumped out of his chair and swaggered out of the room as if he had found a stash of hidden treasures.

"Yikes," Thornberry said. "He hasn't grown any brains yet."

"So it seems." Flint shook her head. "He doesn't know anything. Let's move on."

"Who should I get next? Rick?"

"Yeah."

Flint sat back in her chair as she waited. She heard a muffled conversation, followed by footsteps before Thornberry and the line cook strolled through the doorway.

Rick was a typical kitchen worker in that he had an oversize belly and was, as they would soon find out, very gabby. He sat on the chair in front of the desk with a thud and began talking.

"Holy smokes. I couldn't believe what I was hearing. I was in my usual spot at the chopping block when I heard the gunshot. It was clear as a bell. Don't you think? I've been hunting my whole life, and I know a thing or two about guns. I'd bet on my mother's grave that was a revolver I heard." He stopped short. "Oh, sorry. I guess you have some questions."

"Were both Tim and Kyle in the kitchen when the shot rang out?"

Rick scratched along his chin. "There was a lull in the orders. Kyle stepped out the back for a smoke, I think. Yeah, pretty sure he was outside."

Flint glanced over to her corporal.

"Do you know Stan Kingston from next door?" Flint asked. She sank back into her chair, expecting another long-winded answer.

"Not really. But I've seen him in here almost every day for lunch. Not talking to anybody in particular. I don't think he has any friends. Not that I could see. He always sits at the counter. I could see him through the kitchen hatch. That's how I knew he spoke with Lorie quite a bit. He's a big tipper. Other than that, I don't know a thing."

Before Flint could ask her next question, Rick said, "Oh, yeah. I've seen him at the bar across the street. Shark Cave. Not too often, mind you. But I did see him there on occasion. Handsome guy. You know what I mean. The ladies looked him over."

Thornberry covered her mouth with her hand, holding back a smirk.

"Did you notice who he was sitting with at the bar?" Flint asked.

"No. I didn't take notice of that. Why would I?"

"Anything else you can add?" Flint asked.

"Sorry." Rick shook his head.

"Thanks for your help," Flint said. She handed him her card. "If you think of anything else."

"Right." He stood up, tugging on his waistband. "Stan was an okay guy. From what I saw anyway. I'm sorry he got shot."

With that, he hurried out of the office.

"Whoa!"

"Rick is quite the talker," Flint said. "We'll have to go to Shark Cave. See what his buddies there have to say. Maybe we'll find someone that didn't like Stan."

"Enough to kill him?"

"Probably not."

"Shall I get Kyle in here now?" Thornberry asked.

"Absolutely. I have a feeling about him," Flint said. She held her hands clasped on the desk and waited.

Kyle stood in the doorway and glanced around the room before entering. "I'm kind of busy, you know." He crossed his arms and leaned against the door frame.

"Come in. Have a seat. This won't take long," Flint said as she gestured to a chair.

"Yeah." Kyle plunked down. His short-sleeved shirt pulled up and revealed a barbed wire tattoo that wrapped around his upper right arm.

"Were you having a smoke when the gunshot sounded?" Flint asked, staring at his yellowed fingers.

"No."

"Rick said you were."

"No way. He's mixed up." He pursed his lips into a sneer. "Rick doesn't know what he's talking about half the time."

"Do you know the victim?" Flint let that last question go for the time being, but she thought he protested too much.

"Stan. Sure. He was always in here for lunch." Kyle shrugged. "But I'm not pals with him, per se." He chuckled at his own wit.

"I see."

"I've never talked to him either," Kyle said. He looked at her with narrowed eyes. "Just so we're clear on that."

"Not even once?"

"Nope. But I've seen him talking to Lorie."

"Tell me about it."

"There's something going on there," Kyle said.

Flint leaned forward. "What did you see exactly?"

"I've seen the way they looked at each other," Kyle said. "She wasn't at work on Saturday. Or the few days before." His eyes sparkled as a cheeky grin spread across his face.

"You think..."

"I don't think anything. Go ask Lorie yourself." Kyle jumped out of the chair. "Is that it?"

"For now."

"Yeah, right." Kyle winked at Thornberry as he slipped out the room.

"Thanks for your help," Flint said to the fleeing man. She sank back against the hard surface of the wooden chair, frustrated that Kyle had won round two.

"He's a slippery customer," Thornberry said. She sat down in the chair the cook had abandoned. "Do you think he's involved somehow?"

"Yeah, I do. But I can't put my finger on it." Flint rubbed at her mouth. "He was outside having a smoke when the shot rang out whether he will admit it or not." She was sure she had seen some movement by the screen door of the cafe when she went outside to explore the back of the store property. "It had to be him. There's no one else here."

"He could have seen the killer make his escape," Thornberry said.

"That's what I'm thinking." Flint paused. "But why wouldn't he tell us?"

"He's in on it?"

"Always a possibility, I suppose. We'll keep an eye on him."

"You bet. Should I get Lorie in here now?"

"Okay. I hope she's not as cagey as Kyle."

Lorie sat down and folded her hands on her lap. Thornberry stood by the door.

"Kyle says you know Stan quite well. Maybe even went out together," Flint said. Not exactly what the cook said, but he did imply it.

"He's wrong."

"Oh really? What can you tell us about Stan?"

"He came in for lunch lots. Maybe we talked about the weather and shit like that. I am a waitress, you know. That's what we do," Lorie said sharply.

"Did he ever come in with anyone? Or sit with anyone?"

"No. He was always on his own."

"Have you seen him around town?" Flint asked. "At one of the bars or anything like that?"

"Yeah, maybe."

"Could you be more specific?"

"At the Shark Cave. He was with a couple of guys."

"Do you know who they were?"

Lorie hesitated and looked at the ceiling. "Yeah."

"Well?" Flint was getting exasperated with the waitress.

"Kevin and Paul."

Flint tilted her head.

"I don't know their last names." She glanced toward the door. "Can I go now?"

"Sure," Flint said as Lorie practically ran out of the room. It made her wonder what the waitress was hiding.

Chapter 9

Flint and Thornberry headed back to the station. They walked wearily down the hallway; it had been a long day. With many questions unanswered, it seemed as if they were moving in a circuitous route instead of forward. They heard the rapid typing of keys on a computer as they approached the boardroom. Above the free-flowing rhythm an uneven, almost hesitant, rat-a-tat sound jarred the air sharply. Flint entered the room first to see Jarrett punching at the keys with difficulty as if he only had thumbs. Hay was bent over his laptop, lost in his words, fingers dancing.

"Are you finished with the inventory?" Flint asked.

Both constables looked up.

"No, not by a long shot," Hay said. "We're doing our daily report."

"My typing skills leave a lot to be desired," Jarrett said and continued to jab at the keys.

"It's a burden we must bear." Flint teased him good-humouredly, although she felt tense inside. "Finish up and head home. You too, Thornberry. Get a good sleep everybody. We'll meet up in the morning."

Flint walked down the hallway to her office and sank into her chair, easing into its comfort. She made a call home and spoke briefly to her dad, letting him know where she was. He knew. Then she flung off her shoes and rubbed at her feet before getting down to business.

As the light outside dimmed, she switched on the desk lamp and kept going. A door somewhere in the building slammed twice as she worked on her official account of the investigation so far. She paused occasionally to think through things, staring out the window to an expanse of lawn lit up by the security lights. Beyond that was a blackness broken only by the slow sweep of a lighthouse lantern. In the distance, she could see a whitish yellow glow from the castle. She switched on the rest of the lights to hold back the night, her fear of the shadows starting to creep up on her. The quietness was absolute.

Until there was a shuffle of feet at her door.

Flint looked up startled by the sudden disturbance.

"What the hell!"

"Sorry, boss," Jarrett said.

Flint blew out a breath of air and leaned back into her chair.

Jarrett stood in the doorway, a sheepish grin on his face.

"You scared me half to death. What are you still doing here?" Flint asked.

"I left hours ago actually. I went to the bar for a beer and a bite to eat. On my way home, I saw your vehicle in the parking lot. So I thought I would see what was going on," Jarrett said. "You know I live right up the street."

"Right."

"So, what's going on?"

"Nothing. Merely thinking," Flint said.

"Shouldn't you be home with your daughter?"

"She goes to bed by seven. I missed seeing her hours ago," Flint replied with a sigh.

"This is messed up."

"Are you worried about something, Jarrett?"

"Not exactly." He shrugged his shoulders in a careless manner, trying to laugh it off.

Flint wasn't sure what he was afraid of, probably inexperience was making him jittery. "Are you up to doing something?"

"You mean now?"

"Yeah. Let's go to Shark Cave. Find Stan's friends," Flint said.

"Yeah, sure." Jarrett paused. "How will we find them?"

"We're detectives, Jarrett."

He snorted loudly and followed Flint out of the station to her vehicle. The streets were fairly empty, except for around the pubs and nightclubs. After doing a U-turn, Flint found a parking spot close to the pub. They pushed their way through the throng of smokers hanging out front. The door pulled open easily, and immediately the deafening volume of rock music beat against their eardrums. A few decibels below the racket, a rambling, incoherent jumble of conversations rose and lulled in competition.

Flint lead the way, winding her way through the warm bodies, her nostrils assailed by the pungent smell of body odour, cheap perfume, and spilt beer. Jarrett followed with elbows flung out at his side, clearing a path for himself.

The bartenders all wore loose white shirts with cherry red bow ties and black pants, same as the servers. Every stool was occupied with a crush of people in between. Near the end of the black granite countertop, Flint spotted Lorie Sanders with several men leaning in close to her. One fellow had his arm wrapped around her shoulders.

Jarrett grinned broadly when the sergeant looked his way. Flint's eyes crinkled up at the corners when she smiled back.

Flint barged her way into the waitress's inner circle and whispered into her ear. "Hi, Lorie."

The waitress backed away, pressing further into the arms of her ardent admirer.

"May I have a word with you?" Flint asked.

"What do you want?" Lorie snapped.

"We're looking for Stan's friends. The ones you told us about. Have you seen them tonight?"

"I don't know." She scowled at the detectives.

"Could you try?"

"The blonde guy. The one that looks like a surfer. And the guy with slicked back hair and horn-rimmed glasses sitting next to him." She pointed to a table in the middle of the action. "Okay. Happy now?" She turned away.

Flint followed her gesture and lifted her chin to Jarrett to indicate the way.

Without losing sight of their target, the detectives made their way across the room. When they reached the table, a dark-haired girl stood up and walked away. Flint snatched the chair and sat down beside surfer boy. Jarrett stood behind her, trying to look as tough as possible with his chest pushed out and his arms flexed.

"Hey, she's coming back," surfer boy shouted over the din.

"Is your name Kevin?" Flint asked, ignoring his objections.

"Who are you?" His eyes narrowed as he studied her face.

"Sergeant Flint."

"Whoa!" Kevin held his hands up, palms facing the detective. "You can have the chair."

"Well?"

"Yeah, I'm Kevin." He glanced sideways at his friend.

"So, you must be Paul," Flint said to the guy sitting next to him. She disliked Paul almost immediately. He wore a collared black shirt with a silver vest and very tight black jeans. The sneer on his lips seemed put on as if he was playing a shady character who had stepped out of a wise guy flick. It wasn't working for her. He was a schmuck.

"Yeah, that's right." He said it with a slightly mocking tone and took a large swig of his beer, licking his lips in a suggestive way.

"You're friends with Stan Kingston. Right?"

"Yeah."

"You've heard what happened by now, I'm sure."

"Did he really get shot?" Kevin asked.

"Yes."

"I'm real sorry about what happened to him." Kevin looked from one detective to the other, and then back to his buddy.

"Me, too," Paul said, his contempt for authority shoved to the background. He sank into his chair and pushed his glass around in circles.

"How did you guys meet him? Did you know him from Vancouver before he moved here?"

"No. He approached me at work one day, and we just got talking," Kevin said.

"Where's work?"

"I'm with the town."

"Doing what?"

"Outside work. That's where Stan saw me. I was fixing some irrigation," Kevin said. He looked around the room.

Flint remained silent to let him finish.

"He seemed pretty nice, so I asked him to come for a beer after work." He shrugged. "After that, he became one of the regulars."

"How about you, Paul?"

"Kevin and I have been buds for a long time. He and Stan came to the bar where I work. The Sylvia."

"Okay. What can you tell me about him? Was he a scrapper? Get into any fights? Make any enemies?"

"What? You mean someone who would shoot him?" Kevin asked. "No, that's crazy. He never got into anyone's face. Nothing like that."

"Yeah, I never even saw him talking to anybody, at all," Paul said. "Although, I think he had a girlfriend."

"Do you know the girl's name?" Flint raised her eyebrows.

"No. He never actually talked about a girl. It's just that I could smell perfume on his clothes some nights," Paul said.

"Okay, thanks for your help," Flint said and handed off her card to each of them. "If you think of anything else. However small. Give me a shout."

The detectives left the bar and walked back to the vehicle.

"It's looking more like a robbery every day," Jarrett said. "Nothing personal."

Flint didn't answer. It was always personal, she thought – to the dead guy anyway. She tapped on the steering wheel as she made her way down the street.

After dropping off the constable, she drove on toward her house. It was nearly midnight. She was beyond tired, almost to the point of exhaustion with her limbs feeling heavy. Although her mind was numb as well, she couldn't shut it down. She stopped at the side of the boulevard, switched on the interior light and grabbed her notebook. After searching through the pages, she found what she was looking for. One question lingered in her thoughts. Should she go now, on her own?

Flint looked through the windshield to the few clouds hanging in the deep blue sky. It was a peaceful scene, although she didn't feel the same serenity inside. She reached into her satchel, pulled out a set of keys and palmed them thoughtfully. What could be the harm? She would have a quick look. Get a feel for the man. The place had already been dusted for prints. It was better than tossing and turning half the night. She pulled away from the curb and headed north to a sought-after neighbourhood with tidy houses and large trees. As she neared her destination, she slowed almost to a crawl so she could make out the house numbers. Finally, she spotted the address. It was an end unit of a row of townhouses.

Flint shut off the engine and stared at the house. It stood dark, barely a silhouette against the backdrop of trees. She got out of her vehicle and looked up and down the street. The wind whistled slightly through the dogwood leaves bringing with it an eerie feeling of abandonment. A fine display of flowers lined the brick path up to the front entrance. She climbed the wooden steps and stood on the porch, listening. It felt so desolate. No barking dog, no insomniac roaming the streets of the sleeping town. Except her, of course. With determination, she squared her shoulders and faced the door, pulling away the yellow crime scene tape that was in sharp contrast to the glossy red paint. She held her breath before jamming one of the keys into the lock. But even as she jiggled it forcefully, it refused to budge.

"Damn."

Flint jangled the keys in an effort to find the correct one, almost dropping the entire bunch to the ground. With her second attempt, the lock clicked, and the door creaked open. She stepped tentatively inside, closing the door behind her softly. She didn't want to use the lights and attract attention, so she switched on her flashlight. The bright, narrow beam played with the shadows, creating spooky images on the walls. She scanned the foyer and saw an accumulation of mail under the letter box slot. A quick glance through the pile revealed only junk mail and bills, no personal letters.

As Flint took her first cautious step down the dark hallway, she hesitated. A sweat had broken on her forehead. She would have to turn on the light or just go. It felt so alone. She couldn't do it. There was absolute silence, not even the hum of a refrigerator.

Without warning, a squeak, immediate and loud, broke the stillness. Flint felt a cold rush of air as a large man whizzed toward her, his body bumping into her hard. The momentum sent her into the wall. She felt a sharp sting of pain and hit the ground with a smack.

Chapter 10

Flint had her eyes closed when she was body slammed for the second time. The ensuing shrill outburst of giggles made her head throb. She rubbed the back of her skull, but the small lump that had formed was gone. The fall had made her more frightened than hurt. Another shout. She took cover as twiggy arms flailed about wildly like only a young child can do, a child who missed her mom.

"Okay, okay. That's enough. I give in," Flint pleaded.

The surrender set off another round of laughter as her daughter tugged at the blanket, and then fell back onto the bed.

"Is it safe to come out?" Flint asked from under cover.

"Only if you stay home," Paige said. "Please. You will, won't you?" She sat upright and poked at her mother's eye at the first opportunity.

Flint's heart sank, as it always did when she was involved in a case that took her away for most of the day. But this one was taking up even more of her time. With a sigh, she scrambled out of bed.

"Sorry, honey. I have to get back to work." She gave her daughter a big hug, holding on tightly. "Grandma will get you some breakfast. I'll be there in a minute."

"Okay." Paige screwed up her face, then wandered out of the room, flapping her arms and screeching like a seagull.

Flint managed to stifle a laugh and headed for the shower. It took longer than usual to get ready. Above all, she wanted to escape detection by her father of her follies the night before. Any sign of discomfort, and he would know. Mr. Hawkeye.

From the kitchen came the rich aroma of dark coffee freshly brewed.

"Good morning, Marlowe." Her dad greeted her at the breakfast table with a smile. "How's the headache?"

Flint rolled her eyes and took the mug he offered. She pulled out a chair at the end of the table and sat down.

"Do you want to tell me what happened?"

"It's nothing," Flint answered briskly.

Her dad gave her a concerned look but didn't press her on the matter.

They sat for several minutes sipping on their coffees. Flint was about to defend her actions, wondering how he always knew, but was interrupted by a shrill sound that split the silence. She focused her attention to the backyard where Paige was running in circles after the dog. Her mother sat in a lounge chair watching her granddaughter with amusement. Everybody seemed to be doing okay, Flint thought. Except for her. She stood up.

"I have to get to work. Love you, Dad." Flint leaned in and pecked him on the cheek. "We'll talk later." With one last glance outside, she slipped out the front door.

* * *

The station was quiet when Flint entered. The only thing she heard was the ticking of the clock, no clacking of computer keys, no sound of voices drifting down the hallway. She walked through the empty building and opened the door to the boardroom. She flopped into her chair, feeling exhausted because of her narrow escape from harm. She had been foolish to go in alone. It was a break of protocol that she would have blasted her subordinates for if they had gone that route. And for all that, she hadn't even gotten a look around the apartment. What had the intruder been looking for? Who was he? And more importantly, what had they missed? The place had been processed by the forensic team, a team that she trusted explicitly.

She picked up her phone and punched a number from her speed dial.

"Hey, where are you?"

"I'm pulling into the yard as we speak," Thornberry said.

"Okay, I'm in the boardroom."

"You bet."

Flint heard the front door open and close, then someone walking down the hallway.

Thornberry strode into the room and stood at the end of the long table, her hands pressed palms down on the surface. She leaned toward the sergeant and looked her square in the eyes.

"Where have you been? What have you been up to?"

"I slept in," Flint said. She realized she was coming across a bit deceptive, but she was inwardly angry at her own stupidity.

"Oh, really," Thornberry said. "No, I don't think so. You've been up to something." The corporal stared her down.

"What?" Flint asked.

"When you didn't show up this morning, I asked the others if they had seen you," Thornberry said. She rapped on the table with her knuckles. "And guess what I found out? You and Jarrett went to the Shark Cave pub." She held up her hand when Flint protested. "You dropped him at his house after midnight. He said you were acting weird."

"I wasn't."

"He thought you went home after dropping him off," Thornberry said.

Flint looked up at the ceiling.

"But I know you better than that. Well, what do you have to say for yourself?"

Flint clammed her mouth shut.

"Cough it up."

"I went to Stan's apartment last night."

"I knew it," Thornberry said.

"So what?" Flint said sharply, then relented slightly. "Guilty as charged."

"What the hell were you thinking going to a crime scene in the middle of the night?" Thornberry dropped down into a chair and crossed her arms.

"It's not a crime scene."

"Oh, so that's your reasoning?" Thornberry asked. "But there's more, isn't there?"

Flint hesitated.

"Well?"

"Someone was there..."

"Who? What happened?" Thornberry reached over the table and grabbed Flint's arm. "Are you okay?"

"Yeah. I guess I surprised an intruder." Flint paused. "And when the person rushed out, I got knocked down. It's nothing, really. I'm fine." She spoke quickly, pouring it all out.

"Oh, my God. You could have gotten seriously hurt."

"I know. I know."

"Did you see who it was? What they were doing there?"

"I didn't see the person until they were right on top of me. He was a big guy." Flint shrugged. "I guess we should head over there and assess the damage."

"I'll drive," Thornberry said and jumped up.

Flint followed her down the hallway, her body feeling stiff and sore. She sat somberly as Thornberry drove, wishing she hadn't gone on her own.

* * *

They rounded a curve past a line of giant fir trees and their destination came into view. It was an even lovelier street in the daytime. Thornberry pulled up to the front of the townhouse and shut off the engine. The garden gate was open, swinging gently from side to side.

"My fault," Flint said. "I hope I locked the door."

A gentle breeze stirred the lavender blossoms of a lilac bush planted close by, releasing a sweet, heady fragrance that wafted over them as they strode up the path. Flint hadn't noticed it the night before, but she wasn't surprised. Obviously, she hadn't been thinking clearly, looking straight ahead into trouble. She shook the thought off, thankful she had come through in one piece. That thought lead to another, even less pleasant thought, about her husband. She pushed it down, sighing deeply.

"Are you okay?" Thornberry asked.

Flint put on her best smile and nodded. "Yeah, I'm good."

"The keys," Thornberry said as she held her hand out.

"Yeah, right here." Flint fumbled with her bag and handed over the ring of keys. "It's the gold one."

The detectives entered the house. The place was tidy. The kitchen was spotless. No used mugs or plates on the countertop. The living room was the same, although it was sparsely decorated. No photographs. Nothing personal. Everything in its place, until they climbed the stairs to the second storey. The larger back bedroom was a disaster with drawers pulled out and all their contents dumped on the floor. There was a stack of folders strewn among the socks and underwear.

"What the hell happened here?" Flint asked. "God damn it. What was that guy looking for?"

"I wonder if he found what he was looking for?" Thornberry added.

"Oh, crap. I hope we didn't miss something."

"Like what?"

"I have no idea," Flint said. She pushed at a folder with the toe of her shoe. "Looks like insurance papers, utility bills, bank statements. The usual stuff. Nothing a killer would be interested in."

"I guess not," Thornberry said.

The top shelf that went the width of the closet was bare. All the sweaters and jeans had been tossed to the ground. Suits of every hue hung on hangers, along with an assortment of ties.

Flint rifled through the clothes. "No women's things in here. Check the bathroom."

"Nothing here. No extra toothbrush." Thornberry shouted from the other room. She popped her head into the front bedroom, but it only had a small cot against one wall. The closet was empty.

"Did you find anything?" Flint asked when Thornberry returned.

The corporal shook her head.

"We better get the forensic team back in here and get the locks changed." Flint called Ryan, her forensics guy, but got his answering machine. She left a message and hung up. "Nothing for us to do here. Should we check in on Hay and Jarrett?"

"Okay."

The constables were plugging away with the inventory. They stopped what they were doing when Flint and Thornberry entered the store, anything to break up the boredom. Although Jarrett looked happy enough.

"Hey, Jarrett," Thornberry said. She smiled at him warmly.

"Hi." His voice was soft, a sudden burst of shyness washing over him. He sank his head down a little in embarrassment. His cheeks flushed a rosy red colour.

"How's it going, guys?" Flint asked, glancing curiously at Thornberry. Was there something going on between these two?

"Good. Almost done," Hay said.

"Is everything in order?"

"So far."

Flint frowned. It was looking more like a personal kill, not a robbery. She headed to the back door and stood on the porch. A puff of smoke floated over the fence and landed in her face. She glanced over and saw the cook, his yellowed fingers pressed against his lips as he took a hit on his rolled cigarette, and then tossed it to the ground. His thinning brown hair, tied back in an unfashionable short ponytail, was covered with a tight net.

"Hey, Kyle."

He turned toward the detective. The bright sunlight cast an odd glare on his face, making him look sickly.

"What?"

Flint skipped down the steps and leaned against the fence.

"I think you were out here having a smoke when the gun was fired."

"You think wrong, lady."

"Did you see someone run out the back door?"

"I have to get back to work." Kyle spun on his heels and sprinted up the stairs. The screen door banged behind him.

Thornberry stood on the porch watching.

Flint looked over to her and shook her head.

"He saw something. What's he up to?"

"No good," Thornberry said. She thudded down the steps. "The bank manager called. The video from the security camera is ready for us."

They headed toward the lane, then entered the alleyway. Flint took a deep breath, steeled her nerves and hustled down the corridor.

"Wait up," Thornberry called after her. "What's wrong with you?"

"It smells."

"It's not that bad," Thornberry said.

Flint's cell rang as she stepped back into the sunlight. She answered it at once, relieved she didn't have to explain herself. She was growing increasingly twitchy in the alley, even in the daylight.

"Ryan has been busy," Flint said after she hung up on the forensic investigator.

"Did he get our message to go over Stan's apartment again?"

"Yup."

"Well, anything good?" Thornberry asked.

"Ryan checked Stan's phone first. He doesn't use it very much. There were monthly calls to his brother in Vancouver. Fairly short. He called two shops in town quite often. One was the men's store down on Arlington Road. You know, the expensive one."

"That explains his fancy suits," Thornberry said.

"The other was to the sporting goods store."

"Sports Unlimited."

"There wasn't a number for someone that could be a girlfriend," Flint said.

"Why do you say that?"

"Stan didn't call any number on a regular basis." Flint paused. "Unless the girlfriend works at one of the shops."

"We'll have to ask," Thornberry said. "What else?"

"They lifted some blood from the shop counter that wasn't from the victim, but there was no match in the system. We'll need a sample from a suspect to compare. Ryan hasn't had a chance to look at the bullet yet. It just arrived from the morgue. He's on it now and should be able to tell us what kind of gun it was fired from. But he will need to compare the rifling to determine if any gun we have is the murder weapon."

"Did you tell him we didn't find the weapon?"

"Yeah." Flint nodded her head. "Ryan does have something extremely interesting for us though."

"Oh. What's that?" Thornberry edged in closer.

"He gave the laptop from the jewelry store a cursory inspection and guess what he found?"

"I don't know. What?" Thornberry raised her eyebrows.

"Mr. Altman has some rather curious accounting practices," Flint said.

"What does that mean exactly?"

"He's not sure. He'll get back to us with an answer very soon. But at first glance, it appears Ben is up to something."

"Something illegal?"

"I suppose that's what he's saying."

Flint didn't need any complications with her investigation, but it was in their face, and they would have to deal with it. Off hand, she wasn't sure how it would fit in with the shooting. But one way or another, she would figure it out.

Chapter 11

The tech geek in the bank basement warned them that the memory stick he handed over was the only copy. Flint placed the USB drive into her top pocket and gave a small laugh as if it was a joke. She was pretty sure he had more copies. The room was filled with more cameras, monitors, and accompanying paraphernalia than she had ever seen in one place before. A last glance around made her think there was enough equipment to spy on the whole population of the island.

With the special cargo in their possession, the detectives headed back to the station. Thornberry had grown up in the age of technology and was anxious to see how clear a picture she could squeeze out of the video. She almost ran to the boardroom, her short, chubby legs driving her forward with ease. She fired up her laptop and waited patiently for it to get up to speed. Within several seconds, her email account dinged seven times to alert her to new emails. Ignoring everything but what she had on her mind, she plugged in the stick. A symbol for an external device showed up on the desktop. She clicked on it and sat back as it downloaded the video. The time stamp was in the upper left corner and easy to read. The picture was better than they had hoped, not the grainy crap they usually saw.

"Wow. That's almost panoramic. The guy is good." Thornberry looked over her shoulder to Flint. "Where do you want to start?"

"Is that the beginning?"

"Not quite." Thornberry queued the video. The time stamp registered on the Monday before the murder. "Just like the bank manager said. A full week."

"Let's go to the day of the shooting first," Flint said. "Maybe a few hours after the stores opened."

"Okay." The corporal typed in the date and time and struck a key. "Here we go."

With eyes glued to the screen, they watched closely. People marched by, then disappeared as they entered Shark Alley, crossed the street, or strolled down the sidewalk out of the camera's reach.

"Too bad. It's barely a metre short of the entrance," Thornberry said. She pointed to the edge of the screen where people were sitting on the wood bench in front of the store.

"It's the bank's camera, not the jewelry store's. I could shoot Mr. Altman myself," Flint said. "He should have better security. It would have been nice to get a shot of the comings and goings there."

"It's kind of weird that he didn't have any security. Do you think that was on purpose?" Thornberry looked briefly at the sergeant, and then right back at the screen.

"Not really. I think he's a cheapskate," Flint said, eyes intent on the video.

The crowds came and went, packing the pavement until lunchtime when there was a notable lack of activity. That shifted quickly when the diners spilled out of the restaurants and resumed their shopping. Most were dressed in floral print shirts, shorts, or colourful summer dresses. The picture was so clear they could see beads of perspiration shining on the brows of several people. It had been a record hot day.

"Nothing sticks out for me. Do you see anything unusual?" Flint asked.

"No."

More time went by. The streets got busy again for a while. Shops were closing up as the bars were opening. Then a significant number of young people attracted to the night life filled the town centre, loafing about with nothing to do except smoke, joke around and wait for the night clubs that would be swinging with action in a few hours.

"Hang on. Stop there." Flint held onto her corporal's shoulder. "Back up a bit." She bent forward. "Take a look at that guy by the alley."

Thornberry zoomed in to a tall, slim man in jeans leaning against the wall at the same spot Flint had been only hours ago. He stood motionless, his hands dug into the pockets of a tan windbreaker. A baseball cap was drawn deep over his forehead with the hoodie pulled over his head. All in all, he looked out of place in the hot weather, dressed more for the North Pole than the middle of summer during a hot spell.

"Bingo."

"Have you seen a more suspicious looking guy? There's enough room under that jacket for a Tommy gun. He doesn't need a violin case."

"Start it up again," Flint said.

The man twisted his head slightly before walking out of the camera's range.

"Look. Did you see him turn this way?" Flint asked. "It was only for a second."

"I'm on it." The corporal rewound and played the video in slow motion. Frame by frame, the man moved, just enough. She froze the screen. The detectives stared intently.

"Do you recognize him?" Thornberry asked.

"No." Flint shook her head. "Can you get in any closer?"

"Sure." Thornberry played with the keys, zooming and cropping to the centre of the target until she got the perfect shot. She slid her hands off the keyboard and sat back. "What do you think? Could it be the owner?"

The man had a three-day shadow on his chin, beady eyes, and thin lips.

"Not a chance. This man is everything the owner isn't. Even with all that clothing on, this guy looks skinny. Mr. Altman is short and hefty."

"You're right, but I thought Mr. Altman was up to something."

"Something, sure. But shooting his clerk? I don't think so. No matter what Ryan finds on him."

"Fraud," Thornberry said.

"Oh, sure. But going from fraud to murder is a stretch. No, I don't see it."

"What if Stan caught his boss red-handed stealing from the company?" Thornberry suggested.

"He owns the store. He could fire the guy," Flint said. "You would have to give me more than that to go any further along those lines."

"How about Mr. Altman was cheating the taxman and–" Thornberry paused for effect "–Stan was blackmailing him." She raised her eyebrows, seemingly pleased with her deduction.

"Mmmm. That would explain the fancy suits and upscale townhouse." Flint stared hard at the man stuck in limbo on the screen. "No. I'm still not convinced that Mr. Altman is involved. And really, we have to ask ourselves. Does this guy have anything to do with our investigation or is he another drifter? Are we looking for things that aren't there?"

"Yeah, maybe a drifter whom Mr. Altman hired to shoot his clerk," Thornberry pressed on.

"That seems so convoluted. Don't you think? Where would he meet such a person?" Flint stared at the far wall. "So let's leave Mr. Altman out of it for now and concentrate on whether this guy is someone we would want to talk to. How about that?"

"Okay," Thornberry said.

"The time stamp places this guy near the crime scene at the right time," Flint said, glad to move on to something more feasible in her mind.

"Yeah. Within five minutes."

"Let's check out the rest of the video." Flint sat down and rubbed the back of her neck to get the kink out.

"Okay." Thornberry went to the beginning, set the speed for a quick pace and tilted the laptop so Flint could see better. "That hoodie will be easy to spot."

They spent the next hour watching for the guy dressed for winter.

"There he is!" Thornberry shouted and stopped the video. She checked the date. "Tuesday."

The man stood in the same spot, same time, same windbreaker, but this time he disappeared into the alley without looking toward the camera.

"Keep going."

Three days later, on the Friday, they sighted him again.

"It looks like our Mr. Hoodie was doing a recon of the area. Go back to him on the day of the murder and run it to the end." Flint had noted the time stamp earlier, so she said, "We still have six minutes before the shooting happened."

Thornberry cued back to the spot. They saw a group of women, linked by their arms, strolling down the sidewalk and nobody else until a lone figure entered the scene. "Hey, that's Teddy." She froze the screen once again. "The fireman said he was walking past the jewelry store when he heard the gunshot. So that's it. It has to be Mr. Hoodie."

"There is another possibility. We might be getting hung up here. Maybe the shooter came from the other direction or across the street," Flint said.

Thornberry remained silent.

"Okay. Here's the thing. This mystery guy is definitely someone of interest. I think we should concentrate on him." Flint tapped the screen with a pencil she had picked up and was twirling in her fingers. "Mr. Hoodie ticks a lot of the boxes. Right time, right place. Convenient jacket for hiding a gun. The more I think about it, the more I can see this man could be our shooter. I don't even like the look of his face." Not that an ugly mug could get a person arrested.

Thornberry made a noise of acknowledgement.

"And if he is our man, he's armed and dangerous."

"I'll print a close-up of Mr. Hoodie," Thornberry said. "I'll run off a few of them."

"We'll need a shit load of photos to distribute around the shops. Get a couple of uniforms to tack them up on bulletin boards and lamp posts. I don't know, the bus station," Flint said. "We have to find out who he is. Quickly. Before he catches wind and leaves town."

"You bet."

"It's possible, even probable, that he has already split," Flint said. "That is, if he's the shooter."

"Yeah."

The printer had spit out copy after copy, leaving a large pile on the floor, while they talked. Flint examined the printout the corporal handed to her.

"This is pretty good. Someone will recognize him." She flicked the photo with her finger.

"We need some help to canvass the area. Main Street goes on and on," Thornberry said.

"You're right. I'll give Hay and Jarrett a shout," Flint said. "I'm sure they would be happy to take a break from their inventory tally."

"No kidding." Thornberry snorted a laugh. She grabbed a handful of photos. "I'll run down the hallway and bag a few officers. Get these circulated."

"All right. I'll alert the boys."

Flint dialled up Hay. She reported there had been a hopeful development in the case, and they needed some assistance. After she hung up, they headed out the door to meet up with them at the jewelry store, a little bounce in her step.

Flint felt good about the direction the investigation had progressed. A possible suspect in the wings.

Chapter 12

The two constables waited under the entrance portico, shaded from the heat. Hay tucked in his long-sleeved shirt and hiked up his dark polyester pants as the detectives approached them. He wiped the sweat from his brow with a forearm, even as a few beads trickled down the side of his face. Jarrett seemed completely cool in his white short-sleeved shirt and cotton pants. He had a smile on his face, his usual edginess locked away somewhere.

"Hey," Thornberry greeted them.

"Another hot one on the way," Flint said.

Pyramid-shaped evergreens on either side of the stoop took up a good portion of the standing room, so the detectives stopped half-way up the steps, looking up at the constables.

"Are you guys almost done here?" Flint asked.

"Yes, thank God," Hay said.

"We haven't found anything missing yet," Jarrett said.

"Nothing at all?" Flint asked. "The man's inventory is that perfect?"

"So it couldn't be a robbery if nothing was stolen. Right, boss?"

Flint frowned, not sure if she was pleased with that. Honestly, she wasn't happy with it either way. How many times had she bounced back and forth in her thinking? A random robbery was bad. But a targeted shooting? That could be even worse. She put aside her conflicting thoughts and gathered her team into a tight circle.

"Okay. Here's the plan. You guys take the south side of the street. Thornberry will be on the north side," Flint said. "I'll question the staff at the sporting goods store and the men's clothing shop to see who Stan was phoning. Maybe a girlfriend will pop up." She handed a photo of Mr. Hoodie to each of them. "Now remember, someone may know our suspect and not say because they could be friends. Or they're afraid to be involved. Or afraid of him. So, keep your ears and eyes on full alert for any tell-tale signs of recognition. Are we all clear?"

They all agreed with nods.

"Let's get cracking then," Flint said. And with that, they headed out in different directions.

Flint strolled into Sports Unlimited and immediately spotted a young girl who she thought spent most of her money on clothes. Exactly the kind of gal that someone decked out in expensive suits would fancy. A good girlfriend possibility. She stepped up to the counter and flashed her badge.

"Yes, officer. How may I help you?"

"Do you know a Stan Kingston?" Flint held up a photo from the morgue.

"I don't think so. Should I?" The girl pushed a stray strand of her chestnut hair behind her ear.

"His phone records show he called here quite often," Flint said as she lowered the photo to her side. "Who would he have spoken to?"

"Wait a minute. Is that the guy who got shot? He looks dead. Can I see that again?"

Flint bit back her tongue and held the photo up, pushing it closer to the girl's face.

"I might have seen him in here. Yeah, I think so." The girl stared at it blankly.

The way she said that convinced Flint the girl didn't remember Stan at all. She was being a bit ghoulish, so she asked if the owner was around.

"Sure. Let me get Marianne." The clerk slid out from behind the counter and dawdled down the aisle, disappearing behind a black curtain.

After a few moments, a broad-shouldered lady strode up to the front. She was light on her feet for a person who appeared to be in her sixties and a little on the heavy side. Her smile was warm and genuine.

"Oh, Stan. I'm so sorry to hear what happened to him."

"Did you know him personally?" Flint asked.

"No, no. Nothing like that. A lot of our customers are loyal clients, and we know them by name but not much else about them. People like to be private with their lives these days. Can't blame them. Well, I guess you could say, we know what their hobbies are." She smiled. "Now Stan always bought top quality equipment. He liked to hike. It was only last week, we fitted him up with some good hiking boots. Socks. Bug spray. He's been in the store quite a bit over the summer. Very pleasant guy."

"I see. Are there any other clerks working for you?" Flint asked.

"No. Just our Annie here. She's been with us for" – she swiveled to the girl – "two years. Is it?"

The girl nodded.

"And there's my husband, Ronald, of course. But he doesn't work out front. He does the paperwork and stuff like that," Marianne said. "Oh, and he has a hotline."

"What's that?"

"It's a call-in line for anything to do with sports. What fish are biting. If any cougars have been spotted on the local trails. That kind of thing. So anybody can call the store, and we'll patch them through."

"Would it be possible to speak with Ronald?"

"Sure. He came in a minute ago." She stepped behind the counter and picked up the phone. Moments later, a burly man came trudging along slowly and greeted the detectives.

"What can I do you for?" Ronald asked. "It's about Stan, I understand."

"That's right."

"I'm sorry about what happened to him. He called into the hotline a few times asking about the trails around here. Other than that, I don't know anything." He spread out his hands. "Sorry I can't be of more help." He turned to the clerk. "Did he ever say anything to you?"

"I don't know." The girl shrugged.

Flint tried not to frown. She took the photo of the suspect out of her pocket and held it up. "Do any of you know this guy?"

They all shook their heads.

"Is that the guy who did it?" Ronald asked.

"We're still investigating," Flint said.

"Let me see that again." He put on his glasses and reached for the photo. "No, I can't say that I've ever seen that guy around."

"Thanks for your help. If anyone thinks of anything else, could you give me a shout?" Flint placed her card on the countertop.

"We're real sorry about Stan," Marianne said.

"Yeah. Thanks."

Flint left the shop and walked down the sidewalk and around the corner to the men's store. The bottom half of a Dutch door was closed. She twisted the knob and entered. A large dog lying on a mat raised his head, his ears twitching. His tail thumped on the ground when she walked by. An elderly man stood behind the counter, white-haired and as stylish as a country gentleman. He was dressed in a light green wool suit, crisp shirt, and silk multi-striped tie. He clasped his hands together when he greeted her.

"Good afternoon. How may I help you?"

"Are you the owner?" Flint showed her badge.

"Yes. My wife and I have owned this shop for twenty-five years." He held out his hand. "I'm George. Is there a problem?"

There was a swish of a skirt, and a silver-haired lady appeared from the back room.

"Agnes, this is the police."

"Is something wrong?" His wife stood beside her husband.

"Do you know a Stan Kingston?" She held up the photo.

"Yes, of course. He is a regular client." George paused. "What's going on?"

"Stan was killed."

"Oh my God. We heard that someone had been shot but never dreamed it would be Stan," Agnes said. "How could this happen?"

"So you know him quite well?" Flint said, skirting the question.

"Yes, yes. He's in here all the time. A very elegant dresser," George said. "What a shame."

"What can you tell me about him?"

George glanced at his wife. "He liked his clothes. Agnes, do we actually know anything about him?"

"No. Stan never talked about his personal life."

"Sorry," George said.

Flint held back her disappointment and pulled the photo of the suspect out of her pocket. "Have you seen this man before?"

"He's not the sort that would come in here for his wardrobe," George said. He drew his mouth back into a sneer.

Agnes shook her head.

"Thanks for your help." Flint left her card on the counter. "If you think of anything else." She heard their faint murmuring as she left the store. The dog ignored her.

A warm breeze was blowing from the west. Flint walked back to the main street and stood on the sidewalk, scanning back and forth for her corporal. A wide variety of shops lined the streets, antique stores, luxury boutiques, souvenir kiosks, stores selling leather goods, and an array of restaurants. Thornberry popped out of an Italian shop that sold exquisite purses, her notebook in hand and an exasperated look on her face.

Flint rushed over. "Hey, any luck?"

"Nothing. That was my last stop."

"Me neither," Flint said. "I'm going to grab something to eat before I head back. I'm famished."

"Good idea. See you there in five."

* * *

Flint was the first one back to the station. She stood in front of the white incident board, munching on a pulled pork sandwich. She had already put a name under 'suspects' – Mr. Hoodie. Not really a name, but until they figured out who the mystery guy was it would have to do. After some hesitation, she put Mr. Altman on the board in a separate box. She wiped the goo dripping down from her chin and tossed the napkin in a waste basket. As she was writing a big question mark under 'DNA', Thornberry entered the room.

"Are the guys back yet?"

"Hay phoned and said they were on their way," Flint answered. She swung back to the board and drew lines from the victim to Mr. Hoodie. "So do these two guys know each other?" Flint muttered.

Thornberry sat down in her chair.

The stillness was broken momentarily by the slamming of a door. They could hear loud voices, and then clomping boots coming toward the boardroom.

"Here they are," Thornberry said.

The two constables strode into the room both talking at once.

"Have a seat," Flint said as she continued to stare at the board. "Let me think for a minute."

They sat there in complete silence, save for the consistent drumbeat of Jarrett's leg knocking against the hard metal of his chair.

Finally, Flint faced her team.

"How is it possible that nobody knows this guy? Hay. Tell me you found something."

"We came up blank."

"Did you go to the Seabreeze?"

"Nobody recognized the guy."

"Not even Lorie?" Flint had suspicions about the waitress. It dawned on her that like Paula, she had taken Lorie's word on her whereabouts the day of the shooting. At home. Sick. But was she? Her reflections were cut off by the constable's quick response.

"No," Hay said.

"Any ideas? Anybody?"

"We could put his photo in the paper," Thornberry said.

"We could use social media," Jarrett piped up.

"Perfect." Flint paused. "We'll add a photo of Stan, as well. I'll get it into the paper. Jarrett, you do your social media thing."

Social media platforms were not a language Flint understood, although she knew their power was far-reaching. She gave the constable a wry look so he wouldn't make fun of her.

"Sure thing." Jarrett laughed.

"Everybody go home," Flint said.

They filed out of the room, their shoulders stooped with exhaustion. At the last moment, Thornberry glanced back and saw two more lines Flint had drawn on the board. One from the victim to Mr. Altman. And one between Mr. Hoodie and Mr. Altman. She rushed down the hallway and caught up with the constables as they left the building.

Flint stared at the board contemplatively, her mind not registering exactly what it was she was looking at. Was there a connection between these men? She slumped into her chair and glanced at the clock, realizing she had missed another chance to tuck her daughter into bed.

* * *

The blaring sound of an alarm echoed through the tall buildings downtown, breaking the stillness of the sleeping town. The two uniformed police officers sitting in their parked vehicle on a dead-end street put down their coffees and sat up. Constable Rankin rammed the column into drive and put a lead foot on the gas. The tires spun, leaving a long line of rubber on the tarmac. He rounded the corner and rushed down the main drag as the siren screamed relentlessly. A bright strobe flashed at the front of a building half-way down.

"It's the pharmacy," Constable Jordan said, planting his large hand on the dashboard as he leaned forward.

"See anybody?" Rankin pulled up to the store.

"I'm sure they're long gone. What a racket."

Suddenly the wailing stopped, but the strobe continued to flicker in a mesmerizing pattern.

The officers stepped out of their car and approached the entrance cautiously. The large front window was intact with only a single hole through the glass.

"Looks like someone was having a bit of fun," Jordan said.

"Yeah, right. I'm sure the pharmacist will feel the same."

"That's from a rock, isn't it? Not a bullet." Jordan looked closely at the damage. "Nay. It's from a rock."

"Mr. Glanford is on his way," Rankin said as he hung up his phone. "He was quite startled by my call. Nervous guy."

They didn't have long to wait before the pharmacist appeared on the scene, a sweater thrown over his pajama tops and shoes without socks.

At least he remembered to put on his pants, Jordan thought. Mr. Glanford fumbled with the lock, then stood back from the opening. The officers stepped into the store and took a look around, to make sure nobody was hiding inside. They gave the pharmacist the okay. He rushed toward his locked cabinets behind the counter. With a deep sigh, he sank onto a stool and wiped the sweat off his forehead.

"Thank God the pharmaceutical drugs are intact."

"All right then. Nothing here for us. We'll make up a report. Have a nice evening."

Mr. Glanford glared at them as they walked away, the strobe light still flashing outside the broken window.

Chapter 13

Flint looked into her daughter's bedroom. Paige was wrapped in a deep sleep, her unicorn and rainbow dotted blanket twisted around her slender limbs. Her breathing was scarcely audible – a soft pfft of air as her mouth opened and closed. It was way too early to disturb the sleeping darling, so Flint pushed the soft blonde curls from Paige's face and planted a kiss on her forehead. She felt guilt overwhelm her as she realized not only had she failed her husband, but now she was failing her daughter.

The pale pink sunrise had broken the horizon when Flint unlocked the door to the station. The air was still. It would be stifling by the afternoon. She headed straight for the coolness of her office, sat behind the desk and booted up the computer. Both the local and regional press, along with the RCMP Crime Stoppers website, had splashed the photos of both suspect and victim on the front page. Flint picked up her cell and dialled the RCMP station in Nanaimo where the phones had been opened for callers. The desk sergeant put her on hold while he checked with the constables who were manning the hotline. He came back and told her there were two dozen call-ins already.

Leads to somewhere or nowhere, she thought. After hanging up, she waited for the fax to come through. A buzz and whirl sounded at the printer within minutes.

Flint got up and looked over the sheet. Mr. Hoodie had been spotted on a surfboard, working at a pub, at a party on the beach two months ago, and on and on it went. "Same old shit." She sighed heavily and kept on reading. The second to last call had come in only an hour ago, and finally something looked promising. The person, a Mrs. Hamilton, was positive that Mr. Hoodie had been a guest in her rooming house until a few days ago.

Flint poured herself a second cup of coffee and was staring out the window when she heard the familiar tread of the corporal.

"Hey, boss, don't you ever sleep?" Thornberry asked. She stepped into the room and sat down across from the desk. "I might have a lead."

Flint looked up. "What's that?"

"I went to my volunteer job last night. Every Wednesday."

"Don't you ever get tired of the ragamuffins?"

"I love the kids at the community centre. Mostly teenagers, actually. I have a great time." Thornberry laughed. "After I'm done, I get to go home to a kid free zone house."

"Lucky you."

"One of the kids told me that he saw Stan's photo on the Facebook feed that Jarrett posted."

"Really. So, what did he have to say about it?"

"He said the girlfriend was probably pretty upset."

"His girlfriend?"

"No. Stan's."

"Stan had a girlfriend." Flint sat up straight. "We need to talk to this kid. This could be important. Where could we find him today?"

"At the centre more than likely. It's a summer hangout," Thornberry said. "Do you want to go now?"

"After we check out this first." Flint tapped the fax sheet. "We got a lead from the papers on the identification of our mystery man. Might be solid." Flint stood up.

"Okay."

As they were headed to the east end of town, the sergeant's cell pinged. She glanced at her phone and texted a reply. "That was Hay. They'll be finished with the inventory today."

"Great."

"I was thinking maybe the guys could shake up Kyle. Just a little," Flint said.

"Oh, yeah. Should I get them to haul his ass in tomorrow?"

"Yeah. There's a few people that we need to put the screws on. They're holding back, and I don't like it," Flint said. "Not at all."

She pulled out her notebook and scribbled into it while Thornberry drove. Her cell pinged again. She listened for a few minutes and hung up.

"Ryan went to take another look at Stan's place. Except for the mess the person left behind, he didn't see anything of value missing."

"What the hell was the intruder looking for?"

"Maybe it was a coincidence. You know how empty houses attract the criminal element."

"I suppose."

Flint didn't like coincidences either, but she let it go.

Thornberry parked in front of a two-storey clapboard house with vines running up the siding to the eaves. Large saucer-sized purple flowers covered the lime green foliage. The entire yard was tidy with clipped grass and colourful shrubs. A middle-aged lady knelt among a patch of perennials, pulling weeds and cultivating the soil. She looked up as the detectives approached.

"Mrs. Hamilton?"

"Yes. May I help you?" She stood up and brushed the dirt from her knees.

"We're from the RCMP." Flint pulled out her badge. "We've come about the message you left on the hotline."

"Of course. That man in the paper rented a room from me. He had a scar by his left eye, same as in the photo."

'A scar?' Flint mouthed, glancing sideways at her corporal and shook her head. How had they not noticed that?

"Is he still here?" Flint asked.

"No, I'm afraid not. He left without warning on Saturday."

"Do you mean he skipped out? Did he leave his stuff behind?"

"No, nothing like that. He came by around dinner time, paid up and left."

"Have you got a name?"

"Yes. Casey Snider. He tried to give me a phoney name. I can always tell. Regardless, I make my guests show me their driver's license." Mrs. Hamilton chuckled. "That keeps them honest."

"Yes, I can see that."

Mrs. Hamilton reached into a pocket and pulled out a card where she had written down all the information.

"Terrific."

"Is Casey in some kind of trouble?"

"We just want to talk to him. Thank you very much for your help," Flint said, already backing out of the yard before Mrs. Hamilton started asking more questions.

"Do you think she got it right?" Thornberry asked as she pulled away from the curb.

"All we can do is run his name to see if he's in the system. And go from there."

Thornberry drove back across town to the station. They headed straight for Flint's office and sat down. Flint logged into CPIC, the Canadian Police Information Centre.

Several people named Casey Snider popped up on the screen. They checked the addresses against the one on his driver's license.

"This will be him."

Flint clicked on the name.

"Right on," Thornberry said. "What's he done?"

"Assault. A domestic complaint. And a break and entry."

"Our Mr. Hoodie has been a bad boy."

"He certainly has."

"Check the photo we have," Thornberry said. "I want to see the scar we missed."

Flint brought up the surveillance photo she had saved in a file and enlarged it.

Thornberry leaned in closer. "There it is. The scar. That's really hard to see. That Mrs. Hamilton has sharp eyes."

"Okay. This is our guy. We have a name now and an address in Vancouver."

"Stan is from Vancouver. Did they know each other?" Thornberry chuckled. "I guess that sounds silly. It's a big city."

"There's no phone number listed for him."

"He would have gotten rid of that number anyway. That's what criminals do. They use burners," Thornberry said. "We could phone the RCMP over there and ask them to check out the address for us."

"I have a friend in the east end station," Flint said. She dialled up the number on the landline and put it on speaker phone. Sergeant Lucy Martel answered on the third ring.

"Hey, Lucy. It's Marlowe. How's it going?"

"Hi, stranger. All good here." Lucy hesitated. "Ah. Have you run into Allen yet?"

"What? Why would I? If I saw him, I would run the other way."

"Oh. You haven't heard."

"What?" Flint asked. She leaned back into her chair and closed her eyes momentarily.

"He's your new boss over there in Nanaimo."

"What the hell? I don't know what you're talking about." Flint grabbed the pile of notices in her in-tray, notices she had ignored over the last few days. She flipped through them quickly. "Oh, shit."

"Yeah. Superintendent Hank Parker was in an accident. A bad one, apparently. So Allen Gill is the acting superintendent."

Flint heard a buzzing in her ears and a faraway conversation. All she could picture was the nightmare of that fateful night when her husband had been shot and killed while on duty. Gill had laid some blame on her. For months, the gnawing guilt kept her awake at night. Maybe he was right. But the superintendent's unrelenting pressure was too much to bear. At the first chance she got, she transferred out of his station.

Now he was back. Would the hounding continue? This was a complication in her life she didn't need right now. Or ever.

Flint hung up and rubbed at her eyes.

"Are you okay?" Thornberry asked.

Flint looked up. "Sure."

"So, Lucy will check it out?"

"Yeah. That's what she said."

Thornberry studied her boss, about to say something. But the look she got in return stopped her.

"How about a little lunch before we head to the community centre?" Flint asked.

"Sounds good."

They headed to the Seabreeze Cafe and sat at the counter. The place was hopping with tourists who had heard about the shooting and wanted a look. Paula greeted them, then scurried off with plates of food delicately balanced on her arms. Lorie was either too busy working or she was ignoring the detectives. Flint thought they were most likely getting the snub from the waitress.

Thornberry ate her meal without speaking, realizing something was on her boss's mind. Flint stared with a slight frown at something in the distance, her elbows planted on the countertop. She had pushed her plate away, barely nibbling on her sandwich. "Let's go."

Thornberry swallowed the rest of her coffee quickly and stood up.

As the detectives walked out of the cafe, they ran into Hay and Jarrett locking up the jewelry store.

"Hey, boss," Jarrett said. "We're done here. All kosher."

"Good job, you guys," Flint said.

"We're going to the station to write up our report," Hay said. He handed her the keys to the jewelry store.

"Okay. See you guys later."

The constables walked away. Jarrett turned at the last moment, staring after the corporal, then they disappeared into Shark Alley.

Flint and Thornberry headed to the east end of town and found the kid in question by the bleachers having a smoke. Several teenagers were gathered in a loose circle. They turned around and watched as the detectives approached.

"Peter. Hi," Thornberry said. "My boss has some questions about the photo you saw on Facebook, if that's okay."

"Sure."

"Hi. How do you know Stan?" Flint asked.

"I didn't know that was his name, but I've seen that guy around."

"Okay. And you mentioned he had a girlfriend. What made you think that?"

"They were walking on the beach holding hands."

The other boys in the group made kissy noises and laughed.

"Cease and desist," Flint barked.

"Sure, boss lady," one kid said as they walked away. "Come on, Peter."

He looked at the sergeant with her steely eyes. "Won't be long," he shouted after his friends.

"Sucker."

Thornberry rolled her eyes.

"So you saw Stan on the beach. When was this?" Flint asked as the kids neared the northwest corner of the building.

"A few weeks ago," Peter said, his eyes darting between his buddies and the sergeant.

"Do you know who the girl is?" She had butterflies in her stomach, knowing instinctively that Peter was going to tell her something of crucial importance.

"No."

"Could you tell us what she looked like?" Flint asked, feeling a letdown.

"I don't know. Tall. Pretty."

"Oh." Her feeling of deflation increased.

"What about her hair?" Thornberry asked.

Peter squeezed his eyes. "She had long hair." He indicated shoulder length with his hand. "Redhead."

"You're sure?" Flint glanced at Thornberry, raising her eyebrows.

"Yeah, I guess."

"Thanks, Peter. See you around," Thornberry said.

Peter ran after his friends. They could hear the predictable jeering as he caught up with them, then they disappeared from sight. The detectives walked back to the vehicle and jumped in.

"Are you thinking the same thing I'm thinking?" Flint asked.

"Lorie." She had twigged to the same conclusion.

"Yes, Lorie. I felt she was holding back on something. Now we know," Flint said. "I felt it from the moment I set eyes on her."

Chapter 14

"So Stan and Lorie were going out. How does that help us exactly?" Thornberry asked as they sat in the car talking things through.

"If she lied about that, what else is she lying about?" Flint replied.

"She didn't shoot him. Casey did." The corporal thrummed on the steering wheel, almost as if she was trying to drive her point home. "At least he's our main suspect."

Flint sat in the passenger seat, intently reading her notes on the interview with Lorie from days before, not really hearing what Thornberry was saying. She looked up and asked, "Does Lorie know Casey?"

"Whoa! That's a stretch."

"Is it?" Flint asked.

"I guess that's a possibility." Thornberry looked at Flint intently.

"Why isn't she telling us that she knew Stan? Intimately, apparently."

"I don't know," Thornberry admitted.

"Let's go find out."

"Okay."

Flint flipped through her notebook again.

"Sherman Avenue. We'll have a chat with her landlord first."

It was a two-storey brownstone building with almost no greenery at the front, only a brown lawn and a few wilted annuals in weedy garden beds. Two large big-leaf maples towered over the flat roof from the back. The 'No Vacancy' signage erected alongside the cracked walkway was faded and the paint peeling in large strips.

"Quite a difference from Stan's place," Thornberry said.

"No kidding."

Flint studied the building and caught a glimpse of movement behind a threadbare curtain at a ground floor window.

The glass door at the front entrance was held open by a large rock. They entered the lobby to find themselves in an unappealing and slightly smelly space. The walls were painted in a sickly green undercoat, and even that was peeling off in big flakes. The mailboxes were dented by years of abuse, with junk mail and unwanted flyers overflowing onto the linoleum floor. A door on the right had a large hand-printed sign declaring the occupant was the manager.

Flint knocked sharply on the door with her badge held up in the air. They could hear the shuffle of feet approaching. A shadow passed behind the eye peek, and then the door swung open. A man in a yellowed shirt and grey slacks stood poised ready to retreat back into his hovel. His broad shoulders were hunched over, creating a hump at the back of his neck.

"What?"

"We have some questions about one of your tenants," Flint said.

"I don't know anything about anything." He paused. "As long as the rent is paid on time, I really don't care what they do."

"It's about Lorie Sanders. Does she have any visitors?" Flint carried on as if the manager had not even spoken.

He tilted his head and was about to shut the door. Thornberry jammed her foot into the opening to stop the motion. She had learned over the years that steel-toed boots were best for this maneuver. She smiled.

"Okay. Lorie pays her rent. She's no trouble. No visitors," he said begrudgingly.

"Does she have any friends in the building?"

"How would I know?"

Flint knew better. The manager didn't miss a thing, spied on his tenants. She had seen him move away from his perch by the window. But he wasn't going to tell them anything. And she didn't think anyone in the building would be willing to talk to them either. She took a quick glance around the hallway and decided Lorie would be embarrassed to bring Stan here. Why bother when he had such a lovely pad?

"Have you seen anybody hanging out? Loitering?" It was a last shot to get something out of the guy.

"Nope. I have to go now." He pushed against Thornberry's boot. She released her hold on the opening, and the door closed with a bang in their faces.

"Jesus."

"That was a waste of time," Flint said. "Let's get it straight from the horse's mouth."

"The cafe?"

"Yup."

They headed across town to the cafe, parking behind the building, and entered through the back entrance. Flint looked into the kitchen as they passed the opening. Kyle had his back to them, busy flipping burgers on the grill. They strolled into the restaurant area, surprising the owner with their appearance.

"What's up, Flint?" Paula asked. She seemed a little bemused by their sudden arrival from the back but immediately recovered.

"We're looking for Lorie."

"She's off-shift." Paula glanced at her watch. "She left about an hour ago. Can I get you a coffee or something?"

"No, thanks. Talk to you later," Flint said. They retreated and headed back down the corridor. Outside they stood on the porch, thinking about their next move. "Is Lorie onto us?"

"That's silly."

"We'll catch up with her tomorrow and confront her with what we know," Flint said. "She needs to cooperate with our investigation or else."

"Agreed," Thornberry said as she flipped through her notebook. She stopped on a page and looked up at her sergeant. "We haven't checked out Mr. Altman's alibi."

"Okay. At the least, we need to strike him off our list," Flint said as they headed down the street. "Not that he's really a suspect."

The pharmacy was empty except for the owner standing behind the counter.

"Mr. Glanford. May we have a moment of your time?" Flint held her badge up.

"I didn't think the officers would send a detective to investigate the break-in."

"What break-in? We're here about Mr. Altman," Flint said. She shook her head.

"Oh. Someone broke my window." He pointed to the hole. "They didn't get in actually."

Flint frowned but said nothing.

"It'll be fixed today sometime," Mr. Glanford said. "Oh, never mind. What can I do for you?"

"Did you see Mr. Altman on the day of the shooting?"

"What a shame. That must have been a shock for Ben."

"Monday. Did you see Ben on Monday?" Flint pressed.

"I don't remember the last time I saw Ben. A few weeks ago, I think." The pharmacist paused, looking off into the distance, toward the hole in the window. "Monday mornings are busy, but later in the afternoon there's usually a lull. I would have talked to him if he came in regardless. We've known each other for awhile. No. He wasn't here."

"Have you got video we could look at?" Flint asked.

"I don't have that. We've never had a problem here." Mr. Glanford stopped and glanced at the detectives sheepishly. "Well, except for last night."

"Really." Flint wanted to give him a tongue lashing. There were drugs on the premises.

"I'll get right on that. I'll call my security outfit to upgrade our system. Cameras..."

As Mr. Glanford babbled on, the detectives took their leave.

"Yikes," Thornberry said. "That could have been real bad for him if the burglar got in."

"I'll say. Maybe we should send a bulletin to the shops telling them to get with it. Times are changing. They need surveillance cameras." Flint worried the world was reaching into their small town, bringing bad things with it.

The detectives sat in the vehicle for several minutes before Flint spoke up. "Mr. Altman lied to us. Let's pay him a visit."

Thornberry smiled and started up the engine. She drove to the same neighbourhood as Stan, two blocks over, farther from the centre of town. The trees were even larger here, their canopies meeting in the centre of the road. The lots were larger with bigger houses behind tall fences.

"Mr. Ben Altman is doing okay," Flint said as they drove up a long driveway with deep green lawns on both sides to a two-storey Victorian house. "Real nice."

"I'll say."

Flint rang the doorbell and stepped away from the door. The only sound was the tweeting of birds hiding from the blaring sun in the lush shrubbery. As she reached to ring again, the door opened. Mr. Altman looked dishevelled and in desperate need of a shave. He paused momentarily to stare at the detectives.

"Does this mean I can have my store back?"

"May we come in for a moment? We have some questions," Flint said. She moved forward as Ben backed into the foyer, his face twisting into a grimace.

"I suppose. If it won't take long. I'm busy."

"We'll make it short."

Mr. Altman walked down the hallway to a large room overlooking a huge expanse of grass surrounded by a continuation of the hedge at the front. The lawn was dotted with several specimen trees almost as large as the boulevard maples. In front of the fireplace sat a mahogany coffee table, flanked by four red wingback chairs. He perched on the edge of the closest one, both feet planted on the floor, ready to flee. Flint sat across from him, leaning back into the plush leather. Thornberry stood by the window with her notebook in hand.

"We've come from the pharmacy," Flint began.

Ben's eyes grew wide, and his face paled.

"Mr. Glanford told us that you weren't in the pharmacy on Monday at all. As a matter of fact, he told us he hasn't seen you for several weeks." She stared at him for a second before continuing in a hushed tone. "Can you explain that?"

"I was there when the shooting happened. I went in and out quickly. He didn't see me because it was busy."

"What did you buy?" Flint asked.

"What?"

"What was your purchase?" she repeated.

"I– I don't remember," Mr. Altman stuttered.

Flint crossed her arms and nodded with a smile, a satisfaction flowing into her eyes.

"What does it matter what I bought?" he shouted.

Thornberry stopped writing and looked up from her notepad.

"I was there." Mr. Altman jumped out of his chair. "I don't have anything else to say. I want my keys back."

Flint stood up and pulled the photo of Casey from her pocket. She held it up so Mr. Altman could get a good look at it.

"Have you seen this man before?"

He glanced once at it and turned away. "No."

"You can have your shop back. Thank you for your time," Flint said and handed him the keys.

The detectives left the room without saying anymore. Mr. Altman plastered a blank expression on his face as he followed them down the hallway, not willing to give them a chance to pry any deeper into his affairs. Flint gave him one last look and stepped outside, Thornberry on her heels. The front door closed with force behind them. They got into the vehicle and drove away slowly.

"Do you believe him?" Thornberry asked.

"Not in the least," Flint said. "It makes me think that we should look further into whatever Mr. Altman is up to. Some kind of fraud."

"Or murder," Thornberry responded. "At least, an accessory to murder. Casey and Mr. Altman."

"There might be some connection." Turning to the corporal, Flint said, "But I'll be damned if I know what it is. We'll keep asking questions, see what comes to light."

Chapter 15

By the time Flint was dropped off at the station, it was well past her daughter's bedtime. Again. So instead of getting into her car and heading home, she unlocked the front door and went to her office. She propped her feet up on the desk, leaned back into her chair and placed her hands behind her head. The sun cut through a low cloud in the sky and shone into the room.

Flint closed her eyes and basked for a while in the warmth, breathing deeply as her thoughts drifted, meandering here and there, then landing on the one thing she constantly tried to hide from – that fateful day in the alley. She wasn't even supposed to be there, but they were short of bodies, and she was the only trained officer available. At first, Flint had blamed the superintendent for putting her in the thick of it. Now, she blamed herself for everything that had happened. If only she hadn't been so afraid of her own shadow, it would have turned out differently. Martin would still be alive.

A dull thud startled Flint from her short nap. From her nightmare.

Jarrett stood in the doorway.

"Are you okay?"

No, I froze, Flint thought.

"I'm fine," she said.

"You're sure?"

"Yes," Flint answered brusquely, crumpling a paper from her in-tray and tossing it into the waste basket. "What do you want?"

Jarrett took a step back, surprised with the curtness of her reply.

Flint stood up. "Sorry," she mumbled guiltily. "Are you up for something?"

"Sure. Like what?" Jarrett moved into the room and exhaled a large breath of air.

"Let's go for a ride."

They jumped into an unmarked vehicle and drove to the main drag. After a few passes, Flint steered to the lane that ran behind the stores on the north side of the street. She cruised slowly, scanning each back lot as they passed. As they approached the cafe, she spotted a person strolling nonchalantly, hands in his pockets. The man ducked in and out of the driveways as he moved toward them, eyes darting back and forth.

Flint slowed the vehicle. A hoodie covered his hair and was pulled down low over his forehead. With an upward tilt of his head, the light from a nearby lamppost caught his face.

"It's Casey." Flint thumped on the brakes and jumped out of the vehicle. She drew her gun and shouted. "Police. Stop. Hands in the air."

The man paused for only a second before he dashed down Shark Alley and was engulfed in the gloom.

"Stop," Flint screamed as she ran after the suspect.

Jarrett pulled out his weapon and sprinted past Flint in pursuit of the elusive Mr. Hoodie.

Flint reached the gaping hole that had swallowed up Jarrett. She stopped cold, her fear of the dark cementing her to the spot. Over the rushing footsteps and her own anxious heartbeat, she heard angry shouts erupt. And then, nothing. In the silence and still air, a scream rebounded off the brick walls, clear and urgent. An ominous feeling of dread surged through her paralysed body with that one wail of anguish.

From the abyss, Jarrett appeared before her. His glazed eyes fluttered once. Then he fell to the ground, blood oozing from his shoulder.

Chapter 16

Another day had dawned, bringing with it fear and indecision. Flint sat in her office, staring at her reflection in the darkened window. It was going on six o'clock when the phone rang. She knew the unwanted call would come in early. Although she was afraid of what the superintendent would say, she answered it without delay.

"What the hell were you thinking, Flint? I should suspend you."

Flint tried to speak, but she was choked with tears. For Jarrett, for her doubts, for Martin.

"Well, explain yourself," Superintendent Allen Gill snapped at her irritably.

"I was patrolling the area in the hope of spotting our suspect." Flint cleared her throat. "Jarrett came along with me. We weren't..."

"I read the report. You thought it was your suspect, and then you let your constable go in the alley alone. He should never have gone in alone," Gill sounded off, his voice crackling with anger.

"I was right there," Flint said, cringing inwardly at the pathetic whine in her outcry. She slipped lower into her chair, not really prepared to deal with the coming rebuke.

"This is not the first..." Gill stopped.

Flint closed her eyes for the real onslaught, to the referral of her past digressions. To that night in the alley years before.

"You went to therapy. I thought you had dealt with it." Gill spoke in a low voice, hesitating slightly. "We have to move on, but if it happens again… Well, we'll just see how it goes. Is that clear?"

"Yes."

"Is the constable going to pull through?"

"Yes. Jarrett had surgery on his shoulder early this morning. He's in recovery now." She blew out the air she had been holding in. "Luckily the knife didn't go in deep."

"Luckily for both of you," Gill said. "Unfortunately, the suspect got away."

"We'll get him, sir," Flint said. She sat up straighter, turning at a muffled sound coming from the doorway. Thornberry stood still, unsure whether to stay or leave. Flint motioned the corporal into the room.

Gill hung up. Flint placed the phone back in its cradle and pressed into her seat. She waited for Thornberry to lay into her about her poor judgement. About Jarrett getting stabbed. About what the hell was wrong with her?

"I don't know what to say." Thornberry fidgeted in her chair, ill at ease with the situation.

Flint said nothing and the room went quiet except for the sounds of the ocean drifting through the open window.

Thornberry fiddled with her fingers in her lap and looked down to the floor nervously.

Flint had been expecting a confrontation. She glanced around for a way out. As if. She frowned when she realised there wasn't one. All she could do was own up to what she had done and take responsibility.

"I screwed up. I'm sorry about Jarrett." Flint felt on the verge of tears. "I froze. I think I blanked out for a second. I..."

"It's okay. Shit happens. Forget it," Thornberry said, holding up her palm. "He'll pull out of it. Right?"

Flint nodded, figuring the look on her corporal's face was a little more than concern for a colleague. "Yeah. He'll be fine." But will I be? she thought. The last few days felt as if she was reliving that horrible night. With a deep breath, she fought her way back from the depth of misery and smiled faintly, a strong desire to confide in Thornberry.

A sharp rap on the door saved Flint from making that decision.

A young girl dressed in a flowery green and blue dress stood in the doorway. Rarely did Arlene, the office manager, venture from the other end of the building where she sat all day in her cubicle, the uniformed officers at desks in front of her when they weren't out on the street, and the dispatcher at the communication area in the center of the south foyer.

"Hi. How's it going?" Flint asked. She knew the secretary was happy to get out from behind her desk once in a while and wander to their area for some idle chit-chat.

"Dispatch sent me over. They're having trouble with the internal phones."

"Oh. Have you got something for us?" Flint asked, surprised that her visit was more than a social call.

"Yes. There's been an assault. It's bad. Joe thought you would like to know."

"Why? Send the uniforms."

"He did, but–"

"They can handle it," Flint interrupted, trying not to let her impatience show, but the day was really wearing her down.

"It happened at the Seabreeze Cafe. It's one of the employees."

"What?" Flint felt her heart skip a beat. "Who is it?"

"That's all I know."

A sudden sense of urgency made Flint bound out of her chair, grabbing her keys as she fled. The echo of her footfalls bounced from wall to wall as she hurried down the hallway.

"Wait for me," Thornberry yelled as the door shut.

Flint almost never used her siren and lights. But something didn't feel right. She put her foot to the ground and hauled ass. Within minutes, they reached the lane. Flint screeched to a halt so abruptly that Thornberry nearly crashed into the dashboard. The entire place had been sealed off with yellow police tape where a large crowd of gawkers pushed forward to see what was happening – more excitement in the town. Without any hope of getting through, the detectives abandoned their vehicle and sprinted to the cafe's back lot. An ambulance, the crime scene van, and several police cruisers were parked haphazard at the entrance, blocking their view of the scene. They scurried past the uniformed officers and saw a person prone on the asphalt. There was blood on the man's face and down his body, making it difficult to see who it was.

Flint rushed in. A barbed wire tattoo peeked out from under the rolled-up sleeve. It was the cook. Kyle.

"Is he still alive?" Flint asked the first responder kneeling beside the man.

"Yes. But barely."

Flint heard a sob and looked toward the porch. A lone figure was pressed against the screen door. Paula stepped out and wavered unsteadily before sitting on the steps.

"Thanks," Flint said and walked away. She stood by Paula and asked, "What happened?"

"I don't know. I found him there when I got to work," the owner said. "I called the ambulance straight away." Her voice trembled slightly. "Is he dead?"

"No. Is Kyle usually the first one in?"

"Yes. He gets the fryer going."

"Is anybody else here?" Flint asked.

"No. Only me."

"Are you going to be okay?"

"I suppose. I have to get things ready to open up." Paula frowned and went back inside.

Flint turned back to search out Thornberry. She was standing by the ambulance, watching the men load up their patient.

"What did you find out?"

"All they would say is that he was beaten up pretty badly," Thornberry said.

Flint glanced over to where Kyle had lain, alone and hurting. What was left of the blood had seeped into the cracks of the asphalt.

"There's not much hope the forensic team will find anything useful."

"Probably not. The scene has been contaminated with all the activity."

Without warning, the ambulance siren screamed to life. Flint looked thoughtfully as the vehicle departed with flashing lights, heading east to the hospital. She didn't believe in coincidence when it came to a murder investigation. Somehow Kyle was deep in it.

"We'll talk to him when he gets out of surgery," Thornberry said, reading her thoughts.

Flint nodded, a distant look in her eyes. There were too many things going on that didn't make any sense. A shooting. A stabbing. A beating. Who would get hurt next? And why?

Chapter 17

Lorie's shift started at eleven, so the detectives decided to catch up with her later and really get at the heart of what she knew. It was clear the waitress was avoiding them and doing a good job of it, too. They headed back to the office to do some paperwork while they waited. It had been an early start for Flint, and she was feeling worn out. She sat back in her chair, staring absentmindedly at a file.

Thornberry's cell pinged. After a few words, she hung up. "That was Ryan. He wants to see us in his office."

"What about?" Flint asked. She flipped the folder shut.

"I don't know."

"Couldn't he tell you over the phone?"

Thornberry raised her eyebrows. "He wanted to show us something."

"All right."

Halfway down the corridor, they heard jazzy music spilling out from Ryan's office. When they entered the room, he reached over to the bookcase behind him and shut off the radio, almost knocking a folder to the ground from the overcrowded desk. There was a sofa positioned by the window to catch the view of the ocean, the same view Flint enjoyed from her office. The walls were painted a muted green with framed photos of mountain scenery. It was a comforting space for someone who delved into the most unpleasant of topics, death and sorrow.

"Come in. Have a seat," Ryan said, gesturing to the two chairs in front of his desk. "I have some interesting news."

Flint sat down and leaned into the back of her seat, her achy body appreciating the softness of the leather. Thornberry sat down and clasped her hands together.

"I'll get right to it then, shall I?" Ryan smiled warmly. "I believe Mr. Altman has been up to no good. But you already knew that."

Flint leaned forward.

"I went through his laptop quite thoroughly and found everything looked legit. I went back eight years." Ryan paused and tapped at one of the ledgers on his desk. "But then, I got curious about why he would have hard copies."

"What do you mean?" Thornberry asked.

"Well, usually a person backs up their files on a memory stick. But our Mr. Altman used these ledgers." He pulled the closest one to him and opened it up. "That's when I found the discrepancies."

"He's cooking his books?" Flint asked.

"Yes. The ledgers show he has been in the red for several years, but the files on his computer say he is rolling in the dough."

"So, what's his gig? Is he hiding from the taxman?" Thornberry asked.

"No, I don't think that's it, because he would have to file with CRA digitally. Although I can't be sure about that until I look into it further," Ryan said.

"So, what then?" Flint asked.

"Well, Mr. Altman is hiding the jewelry store profits from somebody." Ryan hung back, studying their reaction to his news.

"And Stan figured it out?" Flint asked. The detectives looked at each other.

"That would be a motive," Thornberry said.

"But there's no one to hide from. He's the sole owner," Flint said. "Something is screwy."

Ryan cleared his throat to get their attention. They both swung around to the forensic scientist.

"There's one other thing. I don't know where the money is."

"What do you mean? You said he was rolling in the dough," Flint said.

"Well, he's got it stashed away somewhere. But at this point, I don't know where."

"Oh, shit," Flint said, wishing something would go smoothly.

"Getting back to this." Thornberry waved her hand over the ledgers. "I think all of this gives us probable cause, if nothing else. We should get a search warrant for Mr. Altman's house."

Ryan sank back into his chair and listened as the detectives carried on their conversation as if he wasn't even there.

"You're right. Whatever the man is up to, we need to find out what that is exactly," Flint said. "But does it really have anything to do with our investigation?"

"Maybe my idea that he hired Casey to shoot the clerk is not so far off the mark," Thornberry said. She smirked.

"I don't know." Flint blew out a large breath. "I think it's more likely that Mr. Altman got caught in the crossfire and is trying to find a way to get out of it."

"What are you saying, Flint?"

"I'm saying somebody's getting swindled, and we happened to trip over his con."

"Everything's so twisted."

"Isn't it though." Flint nodded in agreement, her mind in a twist as well.

"I'll get the search warrant," Thornberry said as she stood up.

"We gotta do it."

* * *

Flint walked slowly to her office and sat behind her desk, staring out the window, waiting for Thornberry to come back. She didn't care about Mr. Altman. All she could think about was the gun. They needed to find it. Everything would fall into place from there. Unfortunately, she didn't believe they would find it at old Mr. Fuddy-duddy's place.

Chapter 18

Flint opened her laptop and googled Mr. Altman. The first thing that popped up was a photo of him with his wife at a fundraising event at the community centre. So maybe the wife had something to tell them. A little more research, and she found they had two grown children. Although Thornberry was keen on Mr. Altman's involvement with the shooting, she was just going along with the old saying: 'Follow the money.' She leaned back in her chair and closed her eyes, trying to fit all the pieces together. It wasn't possible.

A noise at the door made her look up.

"Okay. We're ready to go," Thornberry said, waving a piece of paper in the air. "A couple of uniforms will meet us there."

A police car was waiting by the curb when the detectives pulled up to the house fifteen minutes later. The cruiser followed them up the driveway and parked close behind the detectives. Flint stepped out of her vehicle and spoke to the officers. Thornberry walked up the stairs of the porch and stood in front of the huge door. She looked at Flint to get the okay, and then knocked. The lion's head struck the oak with a loud clang.

Flint looked up to the second story when a shadow behind a window drew her attention. She signalled to her corporal. Thornberry lifted the knocker and let it bang hard against the wood again. This time they heard someone screaming filthy obscenities from within, and the door opened suddenly.

"What the hell? What do you want?" Mr. Altman's face was red and blotchy with bags under his eyes. "I'm busy."

"We have a warrant to search the premises," Thornberry said and held up the official paper.

"No way. On what grounds?" He pushed on the door, but Thornberry stuck her boot on the threshold in time to stop it from closing. "Stop that."

"I'm sorry, sir. But we have the legal right to enter your residence." She held her position until he released his hold.

Mr. Altman wheeled around and fled down the hallway.

Thornberry placed the warrant on the small table in the foyer. She stomped up the stairs. At the top she went right and headed down the hallway. Mr. Altman sat on the end of the bed in the master bedroom. There were several empty suitcases open on the floor. Lingerie and other items of ladies clothing were strewn about the room.

"What's going on here?" Thornberry asked.

Mr. Altman pressed his lips together and glared at the detective.

Flint stood in the doorway with one of the uniformed officers behind her.

"Where's your wife?"

"She's not here."

"That's fine. You'll have to wait downstairs. The officer will accompany you. Please, Mr. Altman. Let us do our job," Flint said.

"What do you want?"

"Please, go with the officer. We will be as quick as we can."

"Don't wreck the joint," Mr. Altman said and marched out the door.

"Right." Flint glanced at Thornberry and shook her head. "I'll tackle the kitchen."

"Okay."

The kitchen overlooked a large family room with a wall of windows showcasing the lush gardens. Everything was spotless as if no one ever cooked. Flint opened the fridge. It was empty except for a few bottles of white wine and an assortment of cheeses. She peered in the freezer for anything out of place. She moved slowly and checked each drawer, reaching into the back so as not to miss anything. The last set of cabinets reached to the ceiling. Flint looked around for a step ladder but there was nothing. She grabbed a stool and stood on it, trying not to spin off and onto the stone floor. The bump on her head from the other night was still sore. So, carefully, she reached up to the highest shelf and felt around. She pulled an ugly green blender with a cracked glass container forward. It looked like it had been bought in the 60s. Flint stretched her fingers a little further and touched something hard with a soft covering. She grabbed it gently. Holding onto the cabinet door, she lowered herself to the floor.

Flint laid the object on the countertop and unfolded the suede rag, one corner at a time.

The Colt 1911 semi-automatic pistol had a blue finish that glinted ominously in the harsh light.

Flint wanted to touch the coolness of the weapon. Her hand hovered over the dark rosewood grip. With her fingertips, she brushed the smooth suede rag flat and closed her eyes for a moment, thinking.

Heavy footfalls pounded down the thickly carpeted steps, and Thornberry rushed into the room. Flint opened her eyes and looked up.

"Oh, my God. Where did you find that?"

"In the cookie jar," Flint said.

"Really?"

"No, it was hidden behind a blender on the very top shelf."

"Is it the murder weapon? Must be."

"I certainly wasn't expecting to find a gun. But it definitely looks bad for Mr. Altman." Flint paused. "But for the love of me, I can't sort it out in my mind." A nagging doubt that all was not as it appeared drew deep lines across her forehead.

"Once we get him to the station for questioning, Mr. Altman will squeal like a pig," Thornberry said and chuckled. She turned to her sergeant to say more, but was caught off guard by the troubled look in Flint's eyes. Her erratic behaviour lately was puzzling. Going to a victim's house without backup in the middle of the night, chasing suspects down alleyways. What else had Flint done that she didn't know about? Flint should be ecstatic about finding the gun. Something was going on, and she wasn't sure what to do about it.

"Are you okay?" Thornberry finally asked.

Flint waved her off. "Don't charge Mr. Altman with anything yet. Tell him we're taking him in for questioning. And especially, don't let on about us finding the gun. Got that?"

"Okay, boss." Thornberry said, baffled at Flint's decision. She headed to the living room where Mr. Altman paced back and forth in front of the fireplace, waiting for them to get out of his house.

As Flint was carefully rewrapping the gun in its soft cloth, she heard a sharp piercing cry coming from the front of the house, and then screaming.

"What are you doing? I haven't done anything." Mr. Altman squirmed in the officer's grip. "You'll pay for this."

Flint pulled out an evidence bag from her pocket, placed the weapon inside and hurried down the hallway. Through the open door, she got a view of the scene unfolding in the front yard. She found to her dismay that an uncooperative Mr. Altman was pinned between two officers with his feet dragging along the gravel. Thornberry stood a few metres away with her hands on her large hips, watching the debacle. The officers released him at the police vehicle. It was a stroke of luck that no one was elbowed in the face as the suspect was helped into the back seat. After several more minutes of hysterics, Mr. Altman pulled himself together and slumped onto the sagging cushion. He fingered them as the car sped down the driveway. Once the vehicle rounded the corner and they were out of sight, Flint stepped off the porch and walked slowly down the path.

"He put up quite the fuss," Flint said as she stood by Thornberry and gazed off, the heftiness of the gun held by her side weighing on her thoughts.

"Didn't he though. Wait until he finds out what we found in the cookie jar. Ha. Ha."

Flint nodded absentmindedly and hopped into her vehicle.

"It doesn't mesh," she muttered to herself.

Thornberry kept her mouth shut as Flint drove them back to the station. They strolled along the corridor to the interview room where Mr. Altman was seated, his back to the door. He swung around and snarled at them.

"You may as well turn around and leave. I'm not saying a word until my lawyer gets here. Because whatever you think you're doing, you're wrong."

"That's fine," Flint said and closed the door. She thought it was all wrong, too.

Chapter 19

Flint only wished she was fine, but she wasn't. She was tired, hungry and fed up with people dancing around her questions. Nothing she could do about any of it except maybe get tougher with the lot of them. She nodded at the guard who sat in his chair outside the room.

The detectives strolled back down the hallway. Along the way, Flint stopped in front of Ryan's office, but the door was locked. She rattled the knob a few times in frustration and walked away. In her office, she sat heavily into her seat and fumed.

"Where the hell is he?" She glanced at the clock. "It's too early to go home."

"Not for normal people. It's after seven and it is a Friday," Thornberry said. "Some people have a life."

"Yeah." Flint sighed, wishing she was at home with her daughter, having dinner, reading a bedtime story. All the nice things that normal moms do. This investigation had sure put a wrench into her routine, and she wasn't liking it. It was at times like these that she really missed her old life with her husband. Someone to talk things through with. Someone to tell you that everything will be okay.

Thornberry sat solemnly in her chair, thinking about other things. She brushed a lock of hair behind her ear and stared out the window. Her dreamy eyes caught Flint's attention.

"What are you thinking?"

"Nothing in particular," Thornberry said and sat up straighter.

"How long are we going to have to wait for his lawyer to show up, for Pete's sake?" Flint struck a pen with quick, light blows against her desk and sighed deeply, glancing at the clock from the corner of her eye. "I'll give them fifteen more minutes, then I'm going home."

"Okay," Thornberry said. She pulled her notebook out and idly flipped through the pages.

"Is this the murder weapon or not?" Flint stared at the evidence bag on her desk. It sat all alone, mocking her.

"Why haven't we got a report on the bullet yet? We really need that." Thornberry looked over to Flint who was rolling the pen between her palms.

"I know, I know. That's what I wanted to talk to Ryan about."

"Try calling him."

Flint reached for her cell phone and dialled the forensic scientist. She tossed the phone on the table after the call went to voice mail.

"Great. No answer." She glanced at the clock for the fifth time. "I'm done."

She pushed her chair away from the desk, then something made her stop. She heard the faint sounds of people talking, and shortly afterward high heels tapping down the hallway. A buxom blond lady somewhat out of breath stood in the doorway. She wore a tight black dress and little else.

"Sorry, I came as quick as I could. I was..."

"No problem." Flint stood up, knowing it was going to be another long night. "Shall we get at it then?"

"Yes, yes. Of course."

Flint strode out of her office toward the interview rooms with Thornberry following close behind and the lawyer catching up in the rear. She nodded to the guard seated at the entrance and entered the room. Mr. Altman had his head in his hands, slumped over the table. At the sight of the solicitor he sprang up to his feet.

"Sit down, Mr. Altman," Flint said.

The lawyer squeezed her way around to the other side of the table. She pulled out the chair beside her client and sat gingerly on the edge, tugging at the hem of her dress. She patted his arm and gave him a warm smile.

"Let's get this going," Flint said. She started the recorder and announced who was in the room. "What was your name again?"

"Miss Klein. But you can call me Joy." The lawyer set her briefcase on the empty chair to her left and pulled out a large folder. She placed it on the table and folded her hands on top. "What's this all about?"

"They're trying to pin something on me," Mr. Altman said. "They searched my house."

"We had a warrant," Thornberry said quickly.

"Are you charging my client with something?" Miss Klein eyed Flint. "If so..."

"Not at this time, but we do have a problem. We would like to ask a few questions," Flint said, "about the incident at his store. We need to clear up some of the details."

"Whatever it is, I'm sure it's probably a misunderstanding," she replied with confidence.

"Sure." Flint glanced at Thornberry. Like they hadn't heard that one before. "As you know, Mr. Altman keeps his own books for his business."

"I'm aware of that," Miss Klein said. "A very successful business."

"Yes. Now here's the thing. We found a second ledger that says otherwise."

"Otherwise?" Miss Klein turned to her client.

Mr. Altman lowered his head and scratched at his neck.

"Please be more specific. What are you saying?" Miss Klein asked.

"Why does Mr. Altman have two sets of books for his store?"

"Okay. I need a minute with my client. I'm not sure where this is going." Her voice cracked, but she continued, trying to go on without wavering and betraying her frustration at the turn of events. "In private."

"Five minutes." Flint shut off the recorder and stood up.

The detectives left the interview room, closing the door behind them. Thornberry struck up a conversation with the guard. Flint leaned against the wall and waited, preoccupied with other matters. Her cell pinged. She glanced at the text.

"Good news?" Thornberry asked.

"Not really," Flint said. "Paige is refusing to go to sleep until I get home. My mom wants to know if I'm going to be gone half the night. Again."

"What are you going to do?"

"I don't know. Nothing I can do about it right now."

The door opened.

"We're ready," Miss Klein said.

After everyone was settled back into their chairs and the recorder was on, Flint started where she had left off.

"Have you got an explanation for us?"

"Yes. It's a very unfortunate situation." The lawyer cleared her throat. "Mr. Altman and his wife are divorcing and... how shall I put it?"

"How about the truth," Flint said.

"Yes, of course. With very bad judgement, Mr. Altman was trying to hide his assets from his wife. Now you have to understand, it has nothing to do with taxes or anything like that. He's not cheating on paying his fair share to the government."

"But he wants to cheat his wife out of her fair share," Flint said, interrupting the lawyer's flow of excuses for her client's wrongdoing.

"Well, if you put it like that."

"I do put it like that," Flint said, her hackles up by the sleaziness of the man.

"I'm the one who worked hard and built the business up while my wife went off on her cheating rendezvouses with other men," Mr. Altman shouted out.

Miss Klein grabbed his arm to stop him from saying any more.

"Did you know about the second ledger?"

"No, not at all." She eyed the detective, a suspicion forming in her mind. "What's really going on here? You're homicide detectives. Why are you interested in some accounting problem?"

"Accounting problem?" Flint sneered, then immediately backed down, realizing there were more pressing issues at hand. "Okay. Let's put that business aside for a moment. We have some questions about the day of the shooting." Flint looked at Thornberry and nodded.

"Where were you when your clerk was shot dead?" Thornberry asked. She eyed Mr. Altman with a steady gaze.

He hesitated and looked to his lawyer for direction. "Do I have to answer that?"

"Yes. Go ahead."

"I already told you. I was at the pharmacy."

"No. You weren't," Thornberry said with a chilling fierceness.

Flint looked on in wide-eyed astonishment at the emotional intensity coming from the otherwise gentle, easygoing corporal.

"Wait a minute. Are you suggesting Mr. Altman shot his clerk?" Miss Klein asked.

"I'm not suggesting anything at this point. I want an honest answer about his whereabouts at the time of the shooting. And we know he wasn't at the pharmacy." Thornberry spoke softly but with the same toughness she had shown earlier.

"I see." Miss Klein held up a finger and leaned into her client. She whispered a few words into his ear and nodded to his reply. "Go ahead."

"Okay. I was at the bank. I didn't want my wife to know what I was doing. You know, with the money and everything." He crossed his arms in defiance.

"All right. We can check with the bank manager," Thornberry said, pleased that she had control of the conversation. "So, to be certain, she will verify you were there?"

"Yes," Mr. Altman snapped. "Is that it then?" He glared at the detective and sort of half stood up.

Thornberry handed the interrogation over to the sergeant with a tilt of her head.

"Now that you have cleared up that little misunderstanding for us," Flint snarled contemptuously. "Can you explain this?" Her voice hardened as she placed the evidence bag on the table.

Mr. Altman inwardly groaned at the sight of the suede rag showing through the plastic. He hunched his shoulders and covered his eyes with his hand, wishing to vanish into thin air.

Flint pulled the object out of the bag and unfolded the wrapping to expose the sleek, well-oiled pistol – the Colt 1911.

"Oh, my God." There was an ugly screeching sound as Miss Klein pushed her chair away from the table. She stroked her neck with a bejewelled hand and swallowed hard. Seeing a gun had caught her by surprise, but she quickly regained her composure.

"I take it you found that at my client's house?"

"Yes, we did."

"Is it the murder weapon?" She regretted asking the question as soon as the words slipped out of her mouth.

"Yes, it is," Flint replied. She sat back in her chair, wondering why she had lied. More like a half truth. It could be the murder weapon. Everything would depend on what Ryan said. She finally chanced a glance toward her corporal. Thornberry was mouthing something to her. It sounded like 'What the f...'

Chapter 20

Flint's cell phone pinged. She glanced at the screen. "I have to take this." She switched off the recorder. "Why don't you guys take a moment before we continue." She gestured to Thornberry to follow her out.

After the door closed behind them, Flint held up her hand and walked away before she answered the call.

Thornberry sat in a chair beside the guard. She pulled out her notebook, wrote a few things onto a new page, chewed the end of her pen and scribbled in another brief observation from the interview. It was easy to forget things, especially when things started moving fast.

Flint put her cell phone in her pocket and looked up, bad news written all over her face. She plodded over to sit in league with Thornberry. Her chair scraped against the limestone floor as she pulled in closer. She leaned forward, and then spoke in a hushed conspiratorial voice. The guard's ears pricked up as he tilted toward the whispers. An intent glare in his direction from Flint made him snap back into his seat and look the other way.

"Oh no." Thornberry drew in a sharp intake of breath and hung her head, running her fingers along her brow.

She glanced at the ceiling, and then back at the sergeant. "Is he sure?"

"Of course, he is," Flint said bluntly.

"So. Now what?"

"Let's wrap this up and move on."

The detectives stood up in unison and marched back into the interview room.

Mr. Altman's disposition was gloomy and sullen when they returned, a dramatic change from his boisterous behaviour before the gun made its appearance. And probably, a talking to from his lawyer hadn't hurt. Miss Klein was young and blonde but not so stupid as to underestimate the seriousness of the situation her client had put himself into. But what he was guilty of was another question.

The detectives sat down. Flint put her finger on the recorder, and then pulled her hand away.

"I want you to speak freely." Flint crossed her arms and sat back, knowing her options with Mr. Altman had shrunk after what she had learned. Thornberry stuffed her handy notebook into her pocket and relaxed into her chair.

Miss Klein eyed the detective with interest, trying to determine if it was a trap. Then decided it wasn't.

"That's fair enough. First, I want to say that my client has not committed any crime. We admit the gun is his, but he does have an up-to-date firearms licence for it," Miss Klein said. "And he certainly didn't use it to shoot his clerk. You're mistaken. It's not the murder weapon." She smiled sweetly, holding her gaze on the sergeant.

Mr. Altman, encouraged by what seemed acceptance of their explanation, lifted his chin in mute defiance.

"You can't hide a pistol in a cupboard," Flint said sharply. "You're not as innocent as you're portraying yourself." Although she was peeved, it had nothing to do with Mr. Altman. But she still wanted something for all her trouble, if only to piss him off. "There are rules."

After several seconds of nervous jittering, Mr. Altman slowly conceded it should have been locked in a cabinet.

"I didn't do anything wrong."

"Why hide the gun so painstakingly if you weren't up to anything?" Flint asked, giving him a proper scolding.

Mr. Altman made a squawking noise.

Flint's lips were tightly pressed together.

"I had the gun in the safe at work, but I thought... I thought if you found it there you would accuse me of killing Stan. So I brought it home." Mr. Altman sobbed. His cheeks were pale. "I didn't shoot him. I swear it wasn't me."

"Okay, if I believe that, tell me something. What was the purpose of having the gun at all?" Suddenly, Flint grew tired of the bantering of this little man and his wily ways. The question she asked was more out of curiosity than anything else. They already knew the gun wasn't the murder weapon because she had spoken to Ryan. The forensic scientist had told her the bullet that was recovered from Stan's chest was a .38 special and a .45 calibre semi-automatic pistol is not chambered for .38 special ammunition so it can't fire them.

"I bought it a long time ago. I don't even have any bullets." He breathed in deeply. "I liked it. I liked having it around."

Flint exchanged glances with Thornberry and shoved the gun across the table.

Mr. Altman pushed into his seat. "What are you doing?"

"You can have your gun back. It's a .45 calibre pistol. Not what we're looking for."

He eyed the detectives suspiciously, tentatively shot a glance at his lawyer and reached for the gun.

"Well, I'm glad that's all cleared up," Miss Klein said as she stood up to leave.

"We're not quite finished here," Flint said warily.

"Now what?" Mr. Altman said, his confidence returning with a vengeance.

"We still have two ledgers."

"We've explained that," Miss Klein said.

"And so you have, but..."

"My client will do a full restitution," Miss Klein looked to Mr. Altman. "Isn't that correct?" She gave him a nudge on his arm.

"I guess."

"We could charge your client with fraud," Flint said.

"And storing a firearm improperly," Thornberry added.

"He will be overly generous," Miss Klein said, catching her drift. She stared down her client with ice-cold blue eyes.

Mr. Altman muttered a sheepish apology and got to his feet.

"Thank you, so much." Miss Klein hurried out the door with her client before the sergeant could change her mind.

"Now what?" Thornberry asked.

"The whole Mr. Altman scenario didn't fit in with our investigation. All he did was waste our time." Flint picked up her cellphone and made a call. After she hung up, she turned to Thornberry. "We have an early morning date. Let's go home."

Chapter 21

The phone call late the night before had been to the owner of the Seabreeze Cafe. Flint wanted to know Lorie's next shift, because she planned on ambushing the waitress. Thornberry accompanied her at seven in the morning, bright eyes and smiling face, eager to get the party going. As they drove into town, Flint steeled herself for a fight. They parked in the lane and headed toward the back door. Flint drew in a deep breath and looked up. The pale blue sky was scattered with fluffy white clouds that drifted easily in the gentle breeze. But the beauty was lost on her.

Flint stormed into the cafe and confronted Lorie.

"I don't know what kind of game you're playing at, but I think you knew Stan Kingston as more than just a customer here."

Lorie glowered at the detective, vehemently denying the allegations. She backed away, bumping against the wall.

"And, you know what, Lorie? More than friends. I think you were dating him." Flint moved in closer.

A chair toppled onto the floor with a loud clank, adding to the tension in the air. Flint swung around and faced Rick who was fumbling with the stool to right it. She saw the quick look he gave the waitress and twisted around to see Lorie shaking her head, her unruly mane of red hair bouncing on her shoulders.

"You knew all along." Flint twirled around again and stared at the kitchen hand for a second before continuing in a harsh tone. "You told me Stan was at the Shark Cave with someone you didn't know. But that's not true. You saw him with Lorie."

"I didn't want to squeal on her."

"I could arrest you for impeding an ongoing police investigation," Flint said.

"Look. I didn't mean any harm." Rick plopped himself on a chair and swiped at the profuse perspiration that had gathered at his temple. "Sorry."

Flint sat on a stool. "Have a seat, Lorie. Someone else saw you with Stan, holding hands. So you may as well spit it out now."

"Okay, we were seeing each other. For a few months." Lorie sat down on the nearest chair and brushed her long bangs behind an ear. Her deep brown eyes under long lashes filled with unrestrained emotion as she stared steadily at Flint. "Please believe me. I have no idea who shot him."

"I think you recognized the photo of our suspect, as well," Flint said, pressing harder. "He's someone you know."

Lorie clamped her lips together. She turned her gaze away from the detective and stared out the window.

"Who is Casey Snider to you?"

For the briefest moment, Lorie hesitated. A shadow passed over her face as if she was uncertain about whether or not to tell what she knew.

"He's my ex-boyfriend."

"Okay." Flint glanced sideways at Thornberry.

There was a distinct groan as Rick shifted his weight in his chair. Paula stood behind the counter, leaning forward with her elbows on the top. She let out a startled gasp.

A sharp rap on the door made them turn simultaneously toward the sound. A large, moon face peered through the window. Nobody moved. The next knock on the door was louder, and then it stopped abruptly. The fireman left, and the interrogation started up again.

"What was Casey doing here?" Flint asked, completely ignoring the short interruption.

"I don't know."

"I think you do," Flint said.

Lorie chewed the side of her cheek before answering. "I guess he followed me here."

"Do you mean he's stalking you?"

"I suppose," Lorie said.

"Do I have to drag it out of you? If so, we can always take this conversation down to the station."

"We broke up and I left town. From Vancouver," Lorie said. She swallowed hard and gave Flint a forced smile. "I couldn't believe it when I saw him on the street last week. He didn't see me though." She pushed her hair away again.

"Is that why you didn't show up for work?"

"Yeah. I figured if he looked around town and didn't spot me after a few days he would leave. You know. Maybe he would think whoever had told him I was here got it wrong." Lorie dropped her head. "Then I would be safe from him."

"What do you mean by safe, Lorie?" Flint asked. "Would he hurt you?"

"Casey is a violent man." She sobbed soundlessly, pulling her knees in tight to her chest. "He scares me. That's all."

Flint rubbed at her neck, trying to organize her thoughts. It struck her that she had been handed a motive. A love triangle. Casey. Stan. Lorie. Was it as simple as that? Something still didn't add up, but she couldn't quite place what it was. Kyle was still the odd man out.

"Do you know something about Kyle that you would like to share with us?" Flint finally asked, trying to get to the bottom of it.

"Sort of," Lorie said.

"That's not much of an answer."

"Kyle told me he saw a guy casing the jewelry store when he was outside having a smoke. Said his name was Casey."

"So, you think it was your Casey?"

"Don't you?" Lorie shot back.

"When was this?"

"I'm not sure."

"So, you think he approached Casey?"

Lorie wiggled in her chair.

"What do you know?" Flint asked.

"Yeah, Kyle said he talked with him on the street."

"When was this? How did he even find out where Casey was hanging?"

"How the hell would I know? Your guess is as good as mine. Kyle has street smarts. He would know where to look. Maybe he followed him." Lorie shook her head and softened her tone. "But he didn't say exactly..."

"Did he threaten to go to the police or something?" Flint interrupted.

"No, nothing like that. He wouldn't."

"So, what then?" Flint asked.

"He asked for some money to keep his mouth shut."

"Okay, let's back it up here, Lorie," Flint said. "That only makes sense if Kyle saw Casey at the store at the time of the shooting." She stopped to let that sink in. "Running away." She said that to emphasize her point.

Lorie paled and began breathing in shallow gasps. She placed her hand over her mouth. "Oh, my God."

"Yeah. That would make Casey the shooter, wouldn't it?"

"Casey is a lot of things, but I don't think he would kill anyone."

"But he would beat the living hell out of someone," Flint said. "Does that sound about right?"

"You think Casey did that to Kyle?"

Flint's cell chirped. She held up her hand and answered. After a minute, she hung up and glanced at her corporal. Thornberry grinned, knowing that the sergeant was closing in on an important detail.

"I'm afraid that's what it looks like."

"Why? If Kyle didn't go to the police, why would he do that?"

"Maybe Kyle tried to go back to the money trough a second time," Flint said. "The phone call I just got was from an officer that I sent over to Kyle's place. They searched his apartment and guess what they found."

Lorie shrugged.

"Over a thousand dollars hidden under the mattress."

"Oh."

"I think it would be safe to say that Casey took objection to Kyle's new demands. Nothing a good beating wouldn't cure." Flint couldn't prove that at the moment, but the pieces were all lining up.

"Will Kyle be okay?" Lorie asked, sinking further into her chair. Gigantic tears streamed from her closed eyes, making thin watery tracks down her blotchy cheeks.

"Let's hope so."

Now that Flint understood what had probably happened, she was counting on Kyle to pull through. Her cell chirped again. She muttered a few words before hanging up.

"What?" Thornberry asked.

"Later," Flint said, pressing her lips together. She sighed, trying to stay positive.

Thornberry sat back in her chair, knowing something was afoot.

"Do you know where Casey is now?" Flint asked the waitress, her eyes watchful of any deceit.

"I never knew where he was staying. Last time I saw him he was driving a van." Lorie wiped her face with her sleeve. "It's white with black paint blocking out the logo from the last owner."

"Okay. That's good," Flint said. "Until we apprehend Casey, I would suggest that you be extra cautious."

"What if you don't find him? What should I do?"

"Go home. Lock the door," Flint said. "We'll let you know when we get him."

The detectives left the cafe and hurried to their vehicle.

"That was a call from the hospital. Kyle might not make it," Flint said, worried now more than ever. His chances of survival were diminishing as the minutes ticked by. Would they have any proof without the cook as a witness? They still had the DNA. She crossed her fingers that the blood found at the jewelry store was Casey's. It had to be, or their theory would be blown out of the water.

"Damn," Thornberry said. "Kyle has to pull through."

Flint could tell by the anguished expression on her corporal's face that they were on the same page.

They climbed into the vehicle and looked at each other.

"What if Casey has already left town?" Thornberry asked.

"I don't think he has. I believe he's too scared to chance being seen."

Flint called in an all-points bulletin and headed to the station to stand by for any news. She filled in more of the blanks on the incident board, while Thornberry called up the hospital to see how Jarrett was doing.

"So far so good."

Flint grinned warily, sat back in her chair and waited well over two hours before giving up.

Chapter 22

The van was found the next morning on a side street not far from the cafe. A team of officers set up a perimeter stakeout and waited for Casey to make his appearance. It didn't take long. A man fitting the description crept his way cautiously in the shadow of the trees, his hoodie pulled low over his forehead. As he approached the vehicle, he cast furtive glances out of the corner of his eye. He fumbled with the lock on the door. As he took one last look around, his hoodie fell away from his face. That was all that Hay needed to get a positive ID. With a quick gesture of his hand, he gave the signal to the others to move in and bounded himself forward with lightning speed. He grabbed the man's wrist and twisted his arm behind his back, leaving him for all practical purposes incapable of moving.

"What the hell do you think you're doing? Let me go." Casey struggled to get free, forcing the constable to pull up higher on his arm. "You're hurting me."

"You're under arrest on suspicion of the murder of Stan Kingston," Hay said as he slapped cuffs onto Casey's wrists.

"You're crazy. I don't know any Stan."

"Kingston."

"Whatever. I didn't murder anybody."

"Tell it to the judge," Hay said as he steered the suspect to the unmarked police vehicle that had drawn up alongside the van. He opened the back door and gently shoved Casey inside.

"You're an ass."

"Fasten your seatbelt," Hay said as he latched the door. He walked down the street to his vehicle, feeling a sense of relief. The arrest had gone smoothly. He dialled up Flint to let her know they were en route to the station with the suspect in custody.

* * *

Down the hallway from the uniform officers, there was a solitary cell with a tiny window high up on the east wall. Not much light got in at this time of day. An officer had unceremoniously put Casey into the small room and left him to fester.

Casey sat on the thin mattress. He rubbed at his wrists and muttered under his breath. As time ticked away, his agitation became more pronounced to anyone who cared to notice.

"Let me out of here," he yelled through the bars to unseen persons somewhere beyond his line of sight. "I know you can hear me. You have no right to hold me here. I haven't done anything."

When no reply was forthcoming, he leaned back against the wall and closed his eyes against the harsh ceiling lights. The glare was giving him a headache.

"You won't get a confession out of me, you bastards," he shouted. "I'll sue the lot of you. I want my clothes back."

An hour later, maybe two, Casey wasn't sure, he was awakened from his light doze by the sound of someone approaching. When they stopped outside his white-walled room, he opened his eyes.

"About time," Casey said and sat up.

"Stay where you are," the officer said. There was a rattling noise as a key slipped into the lock and the iron gate creaked open. "Turn around and back up toward me."

"Yeah, yeah."

With the cuffs back in place, Casey trudged down the hallway, grumbling about his mistreatment. The jailhouse garb chafed his skin and had a bleachy smell. Halfway along, the officer stopped and placed his huge hand on his shoulder.

"Here we are." He knocked on a door, the steel reverberating loudly.

"Come in," someone shouted.

The officer pulled the door open and ushered Casey in. It was a fairly large room with a long table in the centre and several chairs on either side. There were cameras in two corners, one pointing at a chair with an iron ring set in the table in front of it. The other one was aimed at the entrance. The lone figure sitting at the farthest spot looked up as they entered.

"Have a seat." He indicated the appropriate chair.

Casey looked around and reluctantly sat down. The officer cuffed him to the iron ring and retreated. His heavy footsteps faded along with Casey's hopes.

"The others will be here in a moment," Hay said.

Shortly after, more commotion was heard. The two detectives strolled into the interview room and sat.

"Hello," Flint said. With the recorder on, she announced the names of the people in the room.

Thornberry opened her notebook and sat back in her chair.

"Look. You're making a big mistake. I didn't kill anyone," Casey said.

"We have a witness," Flint said, although that wasn't technically correct. Kyle was still unconscious and hadn't told them anything. She had made a lot of suppositions about what Kyle actually saw or knew.

"You're full of it," Casey said. He eyed her up and down.

Flint wanted to slap him. This type of guy always thought they were a gift to women.

"He saw you running out of the jewelry store seconds after the shot was fired."

"Yeah, right." Casey sneered.

"We've sent the clothes you were wearing to forensics for analyzing. So, it won't be long before we confirm that Kyle's blood is mixed in there with the rest of the stains," Flint said.

"Who the hell is Kyle?"

"He's the witness who was blackmailing you, and then you beat him up."

"That's bullshit."

"And we've got you for stabbing an officer," Flint said. "In the alley."

"Wasn't me."

"Your vehicle has been impounded. It's at the police yard. They're going over that as well."

"You won't find anything there."

"We'll wait and see. Won't we," Flint said. She tried not to rub at her face. That would show how nervous she was about everything she had said. She knew he was the shooter, but there was still a long way to go from here to there. The tiniest of doubts played at the back of her mind, but she felt arresting Casey was her only move. Either that or chance losing him altogether when he got wind of their interest in him.

"I want my lawyer."

Flint held her breath for a second before proceeding.

"You can make your call in a minute. Don't worry. I have a few more questions."

"No."

"That's fine, but we'll be getting a blood sample from you first," Flint said. She looked at Thornberry and reached for the recorder. "This interview is over until the suspect's lawyer is present." She pushed the button. "In the meantime, you can stew in your cell until... I don't know. Maybe tomorrow."

"Whatever. I'm not answering any questions until my lawyer is here."

After Casey was returned to his lockup, the detectives headed to the boardroom.

"Go home, Hay. You look exhausted," Flint said.

Although the constable had been around the block several times, having served most of his time in the Edmonton RCMP homicide department, Flint thought it had probably been a while since he had expended this much energy. And he was getting older, fatter. He needed to get back into shape like his buddy, Jarrett.

"Okay. I'm thinking a nice Scotch and soda. Maybe a cigar." Hay chuckled as he left the room.

The sergeant shook her head.

"I don't think there is anything else we can do tonight," Flint said. She glanced at her watch and realized if she hurried, she could get home in time to see Paige. "Let's call it a day. Shall we?"

"I second that," Thornberry said.

Flint's phone chirped. Frown lines formed on her forehead as she listened. After she hung up, she sighed loudly.

"Shit. There's nothing in the van. No knife. And it would certainly be wishful thinking that Casey wouldn't get rid of the gun. But seriously, where are his clothes?"

"Probably in the same place that he ditched the gun," Thornberry said.

"Oh, great. Get Hay on that. Organize a search party." Flint rubbed at her face.

"We'll find the gun and the other stuff," Thornberry said, not really believing that they would. There were a lot of places to throw away unwanted things – evidence. The ocean came to mind.

"I sure the hell hope so," Flint said as they walked down the corridor.

"What if it wasn't Casey who stabbed Jarrett? Could you have been mistaken?" Thornberry didn't want to doubt Flint but was Casey responsible for all the mayhem? The shooting, the stabbing, the beating?

Flint pressed her lips tight and picked up the pace. Maybe she was mistaken that it was Casey who she had seen. After all, Jarrett hadn't seen his face and couldn't identify him. It was too dark in the alley for him to be certain.

"Sorry, just asking," Thornberry said as she stumbled after the sergeant.

"Yeah."

In the parking lot, they parted ways. As Flint drove home, she felt the truth was all there. Just at her fingertips, almost touching it. But then, it slipped away like her good memories of Martin were fading, leaving behind the hurt and the fear. She turned right at the last corner and pulled into the driveway.

* * *

The light was changing quickly. As the sun neared the horizon, the sky glowed a rosy pink hue, casting a subtle hint of purple at the edge of a solitary cloud hovering over the water. Flint glanced up momentarily at the beauty before rushing into the house. She heard laughter floating down from the upper floor. And an occasional shriek. She sighed deeply, flinging off her shoes and ran up the stairs. For a moment, she stood in the hallway and listened to the sound of joy and inhaled the sweet scent of green apples. Flint peeked around the corner of the doorway. The nightly bath ritual was in full force. The claw-footed tub was filled to the rim with a mass of small bubbles. In the centre, Paige sat upright, almost hidden by the froth, splashing and giggling to her heart's delight.

"Hello, darling," Flint said. She smiled at her mother who was thoroughly soaked by the commotion and not caring a whit.

"Mommy. Look at me," Paige screeched. She slapped her plastic duck onto the surface of the water, sending a fresh spray of bubbles into the air.

* * *

Half-an-hour later, Flint closed the book and placed it on the night table. She brushed the wispy strands of hair from her sleeping daughter's forehead and crept stealthily out of the room. Reading Paige a bedtime story was a precious moment for Flint. She felt grounded as she slipped down the stairs and headed to the kitchen at the back. The familiar loud thumping of Bodhi's tail brought a smile to her face. Her mom and dad sat at the table with their evening cup of tea.

"Thanks, Mom," Flint said. She poured herself a cup and sat down next to her dad.

"Is Paige sleeping?" her mom asked.

"Yes. Does she ever hear the end of a story?" Flint laughed.

"Not that I know of," her mom said. "Dale came around earlier and walked the dog."

"Really?" Flint asked. "That was nice of him. I did talk to him earlier. We're taking Paige for a milkshake for her birthday."

"That's sounds lovely, dear," her mom said. "He's a good man."

"It's a surprise. So keep it under wraps."

"Well, I have some things to tidy up." Her mom squeezed her hand.

After Oleane left the room, Flint turned to her dad. "We have a suspect in custody."

"Good. It's been a stressful week for you."

"I hope it's not a harbinger of more bad things to come to our little town," Flint said. She emitted a long, deep breath. "I'm going to take Bodhi for a short walk." It was more for her than the dog. But he was always up for a romp.

At the mention of his favourite two words, the dog's tail lashed furiously on the floor. Bodhi stood up and stretched his full length.

Flint sat on the lowest plank of the stairs leading down to the beach and took off her sandals. The sand was warm between her toes. She lit up a cigarette, inhaling deeply and letting the smoke escape her lips in small rings. She gazed out to sea and listened to the soft waves curling over themselves and breaking on the shore. A slight breeze rustled the overhanging trees on the ridge above her. The pleasant scent of jasmine mixed with the salty air gave her a calm feeling. She leaned back against the railing and relaxed.

The dog dashed back and forth, his front paws taking aim at the incoming tide. Finally, Bodhi came to rest by her side and slumped to the ground.

"Had enough?" Flint asked and rubbed his ears. As they headed up the stairs, her cell phone chirped. She glanced at the screen and moaned, knowing it wasn't going to be good news.

"Is Constable Jarrett okay?"

"Of course. That's not what I'm calling about."

Flint listened for a moment and hung up. "Oh, shit." She glanced at her watch, then dialled Thornberry.

"I have some bad news," Flint said. "The hospital called. Kyle died."

Chapter 23

Flint took no notice of the blue cloudless sky, the warmth in the air, and the fresh breeze that had sprung up early in the day. She barely sensed that she put one foot in front of the other while stomping up the steps of the station and marching down the hallway to the boardroom. She did have a vague awareness of loud voices bouncing off the walls. One in particular rang out above the rest.

Flint rounded the corner and came face-to-face with someone she had never seen before.

She was a young woman, her streaked brunette hair cut fashionably short and her powder-blue suit fitted smart to her slim frame. The briefcase at her side was exquisitely expensive. Her smile was gracious with a slight sneer that curled her lips as she moved backwards away from the sergeant.

Flint pushed past, not in the mood for tedious conversation. It didn't take much to figure out that this youngster was Casey's brief. How he afforded such a lawyer, she couldn't quite fathom, but she was sure that was the case.

The lawyer gave the sergeant a once-over, giving a nod of affirmation that the frumpy-looking detective was definitely the person in charge.

Flint saw the quick glance and wished she had spent more time on her appearance that morning, but she was in a frenzied state of mind. Her choice of the navy blouse was outdated and made her look as dowdy as she felt. She settled into her chair, pushing aside her foolish pride and got down to business.

"What can I do for you, miss?" Flint asked, thrumming on the desk with a pen.

"Mrs. Bedlow. I'm Casey's brief."

Her voice was sweet and melodic with a dry, mocking undertone often adopted by those who lived a privileged life. It grated on Flint's ears.

"See the dispatcher in the south foyer. He'll direct you," Flint said. "Come get us when Mr. Snider is ready to talk."

"Thank you," Mrs. Bedlow said before she flicked a strand of hair and strode out of the room.

"Whoa," Hay said.

"I could hear you all the way down the hallway," Flint said, directing her irritation toward the constable.

"She was snooping around when we got here," Hay said. "I..."

"Why wasn't the door locked?"

"Sorry, boss. My fault. After opening up, I went to my office to grab something. Thornberry came in after." He looked totally embarrassed with red dots on his cheeks and puckered mouth.

Flint's resolve melted quickly when she stared into his puppy dog eyes.

"I'm snapping like a turtle. Let's forge ahead." She glanced at both officers, feeling the loss of her other constable. "What's the news on Jarrett? Has anybody been to see him?"

"They were releasing him when I went in this morning," Hay said.

"Why do they do that?" Flint asked. "Noon sounds better to me."

"Policy. Anyway, he's fine and will be back on the job by Wednesday."

"That's a relief," Flint said. She looked down at her desk, forgetting which direction she was going in.

"Ryan went to the cafe parking lot early and took another look around," Thornberry said, "like you asked."

Flint held her breath for a second, hoping the forensic scientist had found something useful.

"He didn't find anything."

"What about Casey's clothing? Any news from the lab?" Flint asked. "I know that was only yesterday but really how much work do they have over there?"

"Apparently quite a bit at the moment. There's a huge backlog from other cases." Thornberry shrugged. "Summer brings out the criminals in droves."

"Ours is a murder case," Flint fired back, not really listening to her corporal.

"It wasn't when the evidence was handed in. It was an assault case."

"Well, Kyle is dead now. So can't we jump the queue?" Flint's voice rose as her frustration grew.

"I'll phone Ryan back and see what he can do?"

"Thanks," Flint said. "He must be getting sick of me. Asking him to revisit crime scenes. Special favours."

She walked over to the whiteboard and picked up a marker. Her hand hovered over Kyle's name. She didn't have the heart to cross his name out.

Flint looked toward Hay who was sitting silently in a chair. "Could you get a search party going? We need to find the clothes Casey was wearing when Jarrett was stabbed. And where is the knife that he used? There was nothing in his van."

"I'm on it," Hay said.

"And where the hell is the gun?" Flint stopped and gazed vacantly out the window at the rips and eddies in the restless water. "It looks as if he was living in his van, but is it possible he rented another place after he left Mrs. Hamilton's boarding house?"

"I'll poke around and see what I can find out," Thornberry said.

"Lorie better not have been lying about his lodgings." Flint's voice rose as her agitation got the better of her. The more she thought about things, the more annoyed she was with the human roadblocks and slow pace of the investigation.

"I'll have another chat with her," Thornberry said. "Should I phone Lucy at the RCMP in Vancouver? Let her know we got our guy." She glanced at her sergeant who seemed deep in thought and made a note to make the call.

"How did this Casey guy get so crafty? How does he manage to ditch his clothes so well that we can't find anything? God damn it." Flint jumped out of her chair. "Come on people. Let's get cracking. Hay, I don't need to tell you to hunt in the usual places. Dumpsters. Backyards. But make it a wide sweep. Send some constables to the logging roads and check in the bushes along the roadway. Find that gun. Find something. Anything."

Her voice was reaching a fever pitch because they had lost their only witness. Before she said something she would regret, she clamped her mouth shut. Everybody was working hard, overtime, doing their best.

Hay pushed away from the table and stood up.

"Sorry, everybody. Our opportunity to pin this down is slipping away quickly," Flint said. She still wanted to scream but went back to the whiteboard instead, taking deep breaths, slowing her heartbeat down. The answer was somewhere there, hidden among the scribbling and photos.

"Don't worry. We'll get it done." Hay stepped out and practically jogged down the hallway. The loud boom of the entrance door resonated long after he had hustled out.

Flint remained still. A troubling doubt lingered in her mind as she scanned the board for the hundredth time. When she finally turned to face the room, Thornberry was on the phone. After a few minutes, the corporal hung up.

"Well?" Flint asked. "Will Ryan kick it up a notch?"

"It's done, and it's a match. The clothes that Casey wore yesterday had Kyle's blood all down the front," Thornberry said, glad she hadn't had to put any pressure on the forensic scientist.

"And the other?" Flint asked, tugging on her lips. "The blood from the crime scene. Is it Casey's?"

"He'll have those results in a few hours."

Flint lifted her eyebrows.

"He's working as fast as he can. One thing at a time," Thornberry said.

Flint scowled.

"Ryan's words, not mine."

Flint made a noise of acknowledgement. She leaned on the table and tried to think. She flipped a page of the murder book and stared idly at a blank page.

The knock on the door made both detectives swing toward the sound.

"I've spoken to my client. We're ready to clear this up," Mrs. Bedlow said. She walked away abruptly and disappeared down the hallway. They could hear her heels clacking along the limestone.

"This is it," Thornberry said. She rubbed her hands together.

Flint remained subdued and marched to the other end of the building with her corporal in step beside her. She realized this was Thornberry's first murder investigation. No wonder she was so gleeful to interrogate the suspect.

When they entered the interview room, the detectives sat down in their regular spots. Casey was seated on the far side with his lawyer huddled in close to him, cozy like. This time he was dressed in a crisp, blue shirt and jeans. His face was scrubbed. A sexy sweep of thick hair fell over his eyebrows. Flint stared at him flatly. He looked up, and his eyes met hers. A smile formed over his lips. There was something profoundly disconcerting about the wide grin on his face, considering the man's freedom was on the line. Flint looked away, abashed at being caught gawking with her mouth wide open. She pressed the recorder, announced who was present and sat up straight.

Thornberry had her notebook set out on the table in front of her to a clean sheet. She fiddled with her pen, waiting for her chance to put the screws to the suspect.

"How do you know Stan Kingston?" Flint asked.

"Never heard of him," Casey answered without a prompt from Mrs. Bedlow.

"Why did you shoot Stan Kingston?"

"I didn't," Casey fired back.

"Why did you give money to Kyle from the Seabreeze?"

"Don't know him."

"Was it because he saw you running out of the store after shooting Stan Kingston? And he blackmailed you?"

"Nope and nope." Casey grinned.

"Why did you beat him up? Did he want more money?"

"Who?"

"My client has told you he has never heard of a Stan Kingston or a Kyle from the Seabreeze. Have you any evidence to suggest otherwise or can we move on?" Mrs. Bedlow asked.

"Fine. Let's move on to something closer to home." Flint gestured to her corporal.

"Why were you stalking Lorie Sanders? She told us who you are, so there's no need to pretend you don't know her." Thornberry crossed her arms.

"She was my girlfriend. So what?" Casey chewed lightly on the inside of his cheek.

Flint's cellphone pinged. She glanced down.

"I have to take this. Excuse me." She shut off the recorder and exited the room.

Casey pushed his chair closer to Mrs. Bedlow and whispered in her ear. She nodded her head and laid her hand on his arm to still the flow of conversation.

The door opened and closed so quietly that Thornberry looked up from her notebook with a start.

Flint wore an expression of defeat that was hard to hide. She sat stiffly in her chair, pushing on the recording machine once again.

"The blood splatter on your shirt is consistent with someone punching another person. That other person was Kyle. What do you have to say about that?"

"Nothing."

"Did you beat up the cook because he was asking for more money? We found a thousand dollars in Kyle's apartment. If we test the bills, will we find your prints and DNA on them?"

Casey looked at his lawyer. She nodded.

"Okay. I beat him up. He was asking for it."

"I'll try again. Did Kyle see you running from the store at the back?"

"We won't be answering that question, Sergeant Flint," Mrs. Bedlow said. "All we are admitting to is that Casey beat up the cook. It has nothing to do with the shooting. It was merely a disagreement between two guys."

Casey sat back in his chair and nodded in agreement.

"Kyle saw your client running out the back door of the jewelry store right after the shot was fired. What have you got to say about that?" Flint didn't feel bad about the little white lie she had spewed. It was probably the way it came down.

Mrs. Bedlow tapped the table with her pen. "Can I have a moment with my client?"

"Sure thing."

The detectives left the room and stood in the hallway.

"What happened?" Thornberry asked. "It's not good, is it?"

"No."

"It's not Casey's DNA at the crime scene?"

"Nope."

"Shit. So, what do we have?"

"We're ready to make a statement," Mrs. Bedlow said as she popped her head out the door.

"Go ahead," Flint said after everyone was settled back into their seats.

"Okay. Lorie broke up with me. I was furious." Casey hesitated. His eyes flicked around the room before landing on the sergeant's hard stare. He looked away, a hard cast to his mouth. "I heard she moved here and had a new boyfriend. I came here to get her back." Casey glanced at his lawyer.

"Were you going to force her?" Flint asked.

"No. Of course not."

Flint raised her eyebrows.

"I thought if that Stan guy told her he didn't want to see her anymore, she would come back to me." Casey stopped. "She would, you know. She can't get along without a man."

Flint remained silent and let Casey ramble on.

"I went to warn him off. I told him to stay clear from my girlfriend. I didn't shoot him. That's the truth."

"So why did you run?"

"I heard someone at the door, and I didn't want anyone to see me. I heard the shot as I was running down the hallway."

"Did you see who it was?" Flint asked, her curiosity piqued.

"No."

"Are you satisfied?" Mrs. Bedlow asked.

"Yes. The DNA at the crime scene was not your client's."

"Perfect. We'll be on our way then."

"Not so fast. There's another matter."

"What the hell," Casey yelled. "You know I didn't do it, so what the f–"

"Kyle died."

"Ah, shit. That's not my fault."

"Well, yes it is," Flint said. "We're charging you with manslaughter."

Chapter 24

Flint's mom had been calling her all day, reminding her that today was her daughter's birthday. And there was no way Paige was going to bed until she got her milkshake at the Seabreeze. She was skipping around the house, poking in every closet and cupboard looking for her presents.

Damn, Flint thought after listening to her mother go on and on about it. Her dad must have let slip about the surprise. She tried her best to get home at a decent hour, but it was almost seven by the time she pulled into the driveway. She had thought about phoning Paige earlier, but realized quickly that would make matters worse. Milkshake or bust.

So Flint was not totally surprised when she entered the living room that her daughter was curled up on the couch with Victor, the television tuned to cartoons instead of the evening news. Her dad lowered his head and looked over his glasses at her, mouthing 'sorry'. Mom was in a winged chair, ensconced in a romance novel. She put the book on the side table and threw Flint a frown.

Careful not to awaken Paige, suspecting her daughter was actually fast asleep, Flint tip-toed across the carpet and eased herself into an overstuffed chair. She glanced at her precocious child, her blue dress with its white lace collar wrinkled from being worn all day long, waiting for her mom to come home. The rhinestone studded barrette clipped to one side of her strawberry-blonde hair failed to keep the wispy strands away from her face. Her breathing sounded like something between a light snore and a purr.

Flint's cell phone pinged. She glanced at the text.

Paige stirred, then popped her eyes open. "Mommy."

"Happy birthday."

"Is it still my birthday?"

"Yes, darling. Five years old today." Flint stood up and reached to the top shelf of the bookcase, pulling out a small box covered in wrapping paper with a large bow tied around it.

Paige's face lit up. She tore at the paper, letting it drop to the floor and releasing the shiny plastic purse with a blue butterfly for a handle into her anxious hands. She hugged it, then hugged her mom. With the suddenness of youth, she scooted out of the room and hurried up the stairs. A few minutes later a door closed noisily, and then a bang sounded as Paige rushed back. She stood in the doorway, her purse held tight to her body.

"I'm ready," Paige declared.

"What have you got there?" Flint asked, trying to stall the inevitable.

"Money from grandma and grandpa. In case I need it." She jiggled her treasure.

"Okay. Let's go." Flint looked at her mom and shrugged. "We won't be too long."

"Make sure you aren't," Oleane said, shaking her head. "It's her bedtime."

"I know. But I promised."

"You should have come home earlier, if you're going to make those kinds of promises."

"Yes, Mom."

Paige danced down the hallway and was already out the door before Flint caught up with her. She buckled her daughter in and headed out. Dale sat on the bench in front of Altman Jewelry and Diamonds and stood up as the girls walked toward him. He held his hands behind him and greeted them with a hearty laugh, lurching back and forth to keep the present out of sight.

"Have you got something for me?" Paige asked, trying to peek behind the fire chief.

"Maybe."

"Let me see."

Dale handed her a large, turquoise blue beach ball, speckled with glitter and more butterflies. She tossed it on the ground with all her might. It leaped up high into the air and landed with a thunk, then quickly rolled down the sidewalk. The fire chief lumbered after it before it hit the roadway and got away forever.

"Dale will hang onto that for you until later," Flint said.

"Okay."

Paula had been given a heads up with a frantic phone call only a short while ago, so she was waiting behind the counter when the trio trooped into the cafe. She waved them over to the last three stools she had saved for them, placing napkins in front of them.

"Three chocolate milkshakes coming up," Paula said without any dilly-dallying. She turned around and set about making the shakes, knowing it was getting late for the young child.

Flint mouthed a thank you and relaxed for the first time that day. With Paige safely ensconced on the stool between them, and Dale chattering about this and that, she felt truly happy. A sudden whirring sound of the blender drowned out whatever it was the fire chief was saying to her at that moment, his hands moving in tandem with his mouth. She just nodded her head and smiled. She glanced down at her daughter, who watched Paula curiously, resting her chin on her purse that was tightly held to her chest. Nervous and excited. It brought back fond memories for Flint of her mom and herself, so long ago.

Soon the owner placed large fountain glasses in front of them and grinned.

"Happy birthday," Paula said. "Enjoy."

Flint felt a flutter in her heart for the good things in life.

Paige dug into the shake with a complete lack of inhibition only a child could achieve. She sipped the thick drink noisily through a straw, bouncing her shoes off the rung of her stool, content to stay up past her bedtime.

Flint caught Dale up on what she had been doing the last few days. They had not seen each other since the shooting, just a few hurried phone calls. After some time went by, Paige slurped up the last bit from the bottom of the glass and tugged at her mother's arm.

"Okay. You're getting tired. It's time to go," Flint said.

When they stepped outside, the sun was beginning to dip below the horizon. With the light fading quickly, the streetlamps blinked on, bathing the sidewalk in a golden glow. They walked a few paces and stopped in front of the jewelry store.

"That was nice."

"Stay one more minute," Dale said, his eyes sparkled mischievously.

"I'm tired." Paige whined, then climbed onto the bench, leaning into her beach ball, purse close by her side. Almost immediately, her eyelids fluttered and closed.

Flint looked over to her daughter, hesitating before she gave in. "Okay."

Dale ran both hands down her arms. They stood facing each other, close. He moved in and lifted her face to his. She could feel his warm breath against her cheek. His kiss burned hot on her lips. He pressed his body into hers, his hips swaying seductively. Lost in the moment.

A breeze floated down the street, bringing with it the acrid smell of smoke. A sharp, shrill sound rang out. Dale pulled away.

"What the hell? I have to go." He gave her one last brush of his lips against hers and hurried off down the street toward the fire hall.

Flint touched her lips and watched him as he disappeared into the shadows. She turned toward the bench, the shiny plastic purse where her daughter had placed it, still there. But no Paige.

A blood-curdling scream, loud and frantic, filled the night and reverberated in Flint's ears. She froze where she stood, her body quivering. Her skin felt clammy and damp, her pulse quickening, but she was still unable to move. A whimpering cry shifted her psyche. She stepped forward, the all-encompassing fear rising in her throat as she got closer to Shark Alley, to the darkness that awaited her there. Her hand touched the brick wall, holding on, its coolness a sharp contrast to her overheated body. Another whimper made her release her grip and lean into the opening. She took a deep breath to steel herself before plunging into the alley.

Flint got three metres into the gloom and stopped, feeling the pounding of her heart against her chest, the walls closing in. Stale sweat from her clothes lingered in the air, draping her, suffocating her. She tried to swallow, but her mouth was too dry. The heat pressed down in the darkness, overwhelming her senses, sending her into a panic. Choking back tears and nausea, she called out.

"Paige. Where are you?" Her voice trembled. Flint stayed silent a moment to listen, even as she had the urge to shout. Not too far away, she heard a soft sobbing. Then a different sound like a meow. She stumbled forward with shaky steps, deeper into the darkness, driven by the terror of losing her child. Her eyes adjusted as she stared down the alley. Then she saw the tiny figure, hunched over, her forehead on her knees.

Flint pushed through her fear, ran to her daughter, enveloped her in her arms. A cat brushed against her leg. She pushed it away gently.

"The kitty scratched me."

"You'll be fine."

"My beach ball."

"Oh, honey. We'll find it later. Come on." Flint picked her daughter up and strode out of the dark alley, catching her breath, not from the effort but from her own fear. She put Paige down on her feet and kneeled beside her to see the red grazes.

"My purse." Paige struggled to get away, already concerned with other things. She grabbed her purse off the bench, taking a peek inside. "Okay. Let's go home." She yawned.

"Are you sleepy?"

"Nooo," Paige drew out the word. She reached her arms up to her mother. "Carry me."

Flint lifted her daughter, tearful with relief.

Chapter 25

Flint felt absolutely exhausted, both physically and mentally, and wanted to stay in bed all day. Their efforts to find the killer had been stymied by the lack of a DNA match from the crime scene to any suspect. There were no witnesses and no other evidence except a bullet from a gun that was probably dumped down a storm drain or in the deep blue sea. They couldn't pin the stabbing on Casey, because they couldn't find the knife or the clothes he wore that night.

She pulled the blanket over her head to shut out the brightest of the sun shining through the sheers. Muffled voices floated up the stairs and slipped through the crack in the door. She knew it was only a matter of time before her parents lost the argument with their grandchild to keep the noise down because she was sleeping. The exuberance of youth would take over, and consequently result in a shriek that would wake the dead.

The ear-piercing scream coordinated with a rumbling noise as both Paige and the dog flung themselves up the stairs, in the room and on the bed in one fluid motion. Flint was prepared, curled into a ball, head tucked under her arms. The weight of the dog crushed her ribs and pushed her deeper into the mattress.

"Off. Everybody off the bed."

Paige giggled uncontrollably, bouncing on her mother's head. The dog leaped from floor to bed and back again.

"Enough." Flint jumped up, grabbed her daughter and began the tickling ritual. Soon all three were rolling on the carpet in a tangle of arms and legs.

"Down," Flint said firmly to the dog.

Bodhi let out a loud sigh and dropped down on his haunches, his body vibrating, ready to rejoin the mêlée at the first sign of an okay from his mistress.

"Have you had breakfast yet?" Flint gathered her daughter against her and held on tightly, partly in love, partly to settle her down.

"Yes."

"Shall we go and get some breakfast for mommy?" Flint pushed the long bangs out of Paige's eyes and kissed her forehead.

"Yes. You should have pancakes, like me."

"We'll see," Flint said. She glanced at the clock on the night table. "I'll get ready and meet you downstairs. Okay?"

"Okay." Paige squirmed out of her arms and flew down the stairs. "Mommy wants pancakes."

Flint shook her head in mock despair, then stepped into the shower. Twenty minutes later, she set foot into the kitchen, fully expecting to find a hive of activity. Instead, all surfaces were cleared of dishes, the dishwasher hummed through its cycle, and her dad sat calmly at the head of the table. She looked out the large window toward the ocean. Her mother and daughter were down by the water with the dog barking and running circles around them.

"Hello, sweetheart." Victor rose and refilled his mug and gave a filled one to Flint.

"Hi, Dad." She sat down.

"Shall I scramble some eggs for you," Victor asked.

"No. I'm good." Flint sighed, her anxiety showing in the way she gritted her teeth and tugged on her ear.

"Is your investigation going poorly?"

"Yeah. We've run out of suspects," Flint said, "and no motive for the shooting. Everyone seems to have liked the victim. I guess it's an armed robbery gone wrong, just like my junior constable said."

"Not everything has a purpose."

"I guess." Flint stood up. "I'm running late. Got to go."

"You're doing fine," Victor said.

"Thanks, Dad," Flint said. His insight into her feelings were always spot on. "We'll talk."

* * *

Flint entered the station and headed straight to the boardroom. It was empty. She walked down the hallway and checked all of the offices. It was as if everyone had abandoned her, not a soul in sight. She walked back to her office and flopped into her chair. After flipping through a couple of files, she gave up and tossed the folder onto her desk. She didn't know what she was looking for. Should she review the video tape again? Interview everyone again? And ask what? Why hadn't she run out the back door of the store and given chase when she heard the shot? She had been too cautious, creeping into the store as if the shooter was waiting for the police to arrive.

It was too late to second guess her moves. She had followed protocol. In the good old days, before Martin was killed, she would have thrown caution to the wind. On the positive side, last night had been a step in the right direction. She had overcome her fear of the dark to rescue her daughter. Would she be able to do it again?

Flint lowered her head to her chest and sobbed. A slight noise at the door made her look away and swipe at her eyes with the back of her hand.

"Are you okay, Flint?" Thornberry asked. She entered the room and sat down in front of the desk. "Can I do something?"

"I'm fine," Flint said. "I was feeling a little overwhelmed. It'll pass."

"Hay found the knife," Thornberry said.

"What? Where?" Flint sat up and leaned forward.

"Well, a knife. But he thinks it's the knife Casey used on Jarrett," Thornberry said. "In the bin at the Seabreeze."

"Oh, shit. You're kidding me?" Flint stuck her tongue out. "That must have been nauseating."

"Yeah. He said he showered twice trying to get the stink out." Thornberry laughed at the thought. "Good news is there's blood on it. Ryan is at the lab doing the tests. He said he'll use the rapid DNA to get us the results quickly."

"When will we hear?" Flint asked.

"Any moment now," Thornberry said. She picked up her cell phone and glanced at the screen. "Oh yeah, I forgot to tell you. Jarrett said he was so bored one day that he googled Casey."

"Did he find anything interesting?"

"His dad is some big hotshot in Alberta. Oilfields. Mr. Megabucks," Thornberry said. "It explains where he gets his money from."

"That it does."

"Well, Casey won't be able to spend it where he's going," Thornberry said.

"It'll piss me off if his dad manages to bail him out of this mess." Flint shook her head.

"Nah, Casey's in too deep."

A noise in the hallway caught their attention. Heavy footfalls sounded as someone approached the office, then heavier breathing as Hay rounded the corner and popped his head around the doorway.

"We got him. A clear set of Casey's prints on the handle and Jarrett's blood on the blade. Yahoo!" Hay flopped himself into a chair and wiped his brow. "I phoned Jarrett already and told him the good news."

"Fantastic. Excellent work," Flint said, wrinkling her nose at him.

"Nice. After all I did," Hay said.

"You're a hero." Flint smiled at the constable. "Now the best part. Could you call up Mrs. Bedlow and tell her we'll be adding a new charge against her client. Assault on a police officer."

"My pleasure," Hay said.

"That'll add a few more years to Casey's free room and board," Thornberry said. "He deserves it."

"What made you look there?" Flint asked the constable.

"We looked everywhere else. I was having a coffee and thought what the heck." Hay grinned.

"When was garbage day?"

"Today for that bin. They rotate them."

"Whoa. Lucky," Flint said.

They sat in silence looking at each other.

"What's next?" Thornberry asked.

"I'm not sure. Everybody loved Stan, apparently. So…"

"I can run his name through CPIC, the Canadian Police Identification Centre," Hay said, "for something to do." He shrugged. "I guess that's a stupid idea."

"I don't see how that will help, but go ahead fill your boots," Flint said.

Hay flipped open his laptop and logged into the RCMP website. He clicked on the name. "Okay. I see a DUI." He scrolled down the page. "Non-conviction. That's it."

"That isn't much help," Thornberry said.

"Any more ideas anybody?" Flint asked.

Chapter 26

The sound of ocean waves crashing and seagulls squalling in the spray could be heard during lulls in the conversation. The sporadic exchange of ideas brought them no closer to how to move forward. They had pulled out all the stops to find the shooter, but they couldn't link the DNA at the crime scene to anyone. They had run out of suspects. And the missing gun was a huge sticking point. Without it they really had nothing. The clock on the wall crawled slowly forward, even as the investigation ground to a halt.

The only sensible suggestion was to go for lunch. Flint's mood lifted momentarily, but it didn't last. She was anxious to get back to the station. There was a task she had been putting off, but she knew time was almost up.

Back in the boardroom, they began where they had left off.

"Why? There doesn't seem to be a why," Flint said. She stared at the whiteboard.

The room had gone quiet. The only real noise was the gurgling of the coffee maker someone had switched on when they had returned.

After a few seconds of dead air, Thornberry spoke up. "We could talk to Lorie again."

"Sure. Why not? Seeing as she is our only connection to Stan." Flint tapped the folder in front of her. "Let's bring her into the station. Hay, would you handle that?"

"Sure. She was at work this morning. Should still be there." He slipped out of the room.

"Not looking forward to this conversation." Flint picked up her cellphone. "The super will be expecting an update. I would rather call him before he rings me up."

"Don't blame you," Thornberry said. "We're doing all we can–"

"Yeah, yeah." Flint dialled the superintendent and waited to be put through to his office. She held the phone away from her ear a few times and rolled her eyes. At the end, she nodded and hung up with a cheery 'talk to you later'.

"What did he have to say?"

"I'm surprised how nice he was about it all. Said we did good work getting Casey off the streets."

"That's a good sign."

"He said not to be discouraged that we didn't arrest anyone for the shooting. Not all cases get solved."

"True enough, but I really wanted to close this case," Thornberry said. She sighed.

"Me too," Flint said. "Interesting though, after I told him about the DUI, he suggested we get a criminal record synopsis."

"But he wasn't convicted of anything."

"That's what I told him. Gill said it doesn't matter. It'll give us all the details about the charge and disposition information including non-convictions."

"Okay. What good will that do?" Thornberry asked.

"Not sure, but it would make Gill happy," Flint said. "Nothing wrong with staying on the right side of the boss."

"The super is warming up to you." Thornberry laughed. She ducked at Flint's punch. "I'll write up the request right now."

After she left, Flint went to the boardroom and stared at the whiteboard. She rubbed off Casey and Mr. Altman's names. She spent the next hour going through the interview transcripts. When she picked up Kyle's folder, she blew out a breath and returned it to the box. She was scrutinizing Lorie's file when she heard murmurs coming from the front entrance. There was the sound of heavy footfalls, followed by another pair of feet pattering quickly behind. The mezzo-soprano tone rang out above the deeply gruff voice of her constable.

* * *

Lorie Sanders's alabaster skin held a rosy glow that had been missing when Flint first met her. Obviously, she had heard the good news that Casey was locked away. She could finally walk down the street without looking over her shoulder.

"Have a seat." Flint gestured to a chair. "Feeling better?"

"What a relief," Lorie said. "How long?" She drew in a deep breath, a flash of anxiety crossing her face.

"A long time. You don't need to fret," Flint said. "Now, we need to ask a few more questions about Stan."

Flint rummaged in the top drawer of her desk. She pulled out a set of keys, separating one from the ring.

"Stan and you exchanged apartment keys. Isn't that so?"

"Aah, I guess." Lorie looked like she was going to say more but stopped herself.

Flint narrowed her eyes.

"It was serious," Lorie finally said.

"I'm sorry for your loss." Flint sat back in her chair.

"We really liked each other. I think he was the one." Lorie paled and twisted her hands together. After a long pause, she said, "We saw each other four or five times a week."

"There were no phone calls between the two of you. How did you make arrangements?" Flint asked.

"You checked my phone?" Her voice had drawn tight with contained anger.

"Normal procedure during an investigation," Flint said. "So, what was the setup?"

"Nothing nefarious, if that's what you're thinking," Lorie said, and then relenting. "We're private people."

"Okay."

Lorie sighed. "Stan came in for lunch on days he was free in the evening. That's when we would agree on a time. We always went to his place." Lorie shrugged. "It was a real nice apartment not like my dump."

Flint nodded her head. She had seen both places.

"He didn't talk about his past much," Lorie said. "Maybe Teddy could help with that."

"Our Teddy. The fireman?"

"Yes."

Flint lifted her chin at Hay. He knew the drill and headed out, pushing past Thornberry who was on her way in.

"I've sent the request," Thornberry said. She stood in the doorway for a second before taking a seat across from the waitress.

"Have you got a timeline for a reply?" Flint asked, turning away from the waitress.

"We'll get it tomorrow. They're so not busy."

"Perfect. Lorie tells us that Stan and Teddy were friends," Flint said. "Is that what you're saying, Lorie?"

"I don't know if they're friends exactly. They went to the same college."

"How come we didn't know this?" Thornberry asked. She leaned across the table. "Why didn't you tell us this before? How many times did I talk to you? Shit." She sank back into her chair. "We should charge Miss Sanders with obstruction of justice or something..."

"Enough." Flint held up her hand.

"What bullshit."

After Thornberry cooled down, Flint continued. "Why didn't you mention this before?"

Lorie looked out the window, then back at the sergeant.

"I didn't want to explain myself. Get the third degree because I was seeing Stan. My life is complicated enough."

"You have caused us quite a bit of trouble," Flint said. She almost spouted out that Lorie had possibly got Kyle killed, but that would have been downright cruel.

"Was it my fault that..." The rosy colour on Lorie's face drained away, slowly and completely, with the realization of what she might have caused. "Kyle..."

"Don't go there," Flint said. "Just tell us if there is anything else that you know about Stan. Think carefully. Did he mention anybody he was afraid of? Or that he had done something to anger someone? Someone that wanted revenge?"

She stopped, realizing she was grasping at straws now. Why couldn't she let it go? A young respectable man like Stan didn't have enemies. Maybe a woman scorned.

"Everyone liked Stan. He was a nice guy." Lorie paused. "He missed his parents, I know that." She struggled with the words. "It was a new start for both of us. We talked about the future."

She leaned forward onto her elbows and buried her face in her hands. Her resolve crumbled and tears began to stream silently down her cheeks.

Flint and Thornberry exchanged glances. The sergeant mouthed 'get her home'.

With some effort, Lorie looked up when the corporal touched her arm. Her face was reddened and blotchy from crying. The muscle in her jaw clenched, and Flint could tell she was trying hard not to start up again. It made the sergeant feel bad that she had relentlessly hammered away at the waitress with questions and accusations. But she had no choice when a witness was not forthcoming. Now with the new information, she was anxious to hear what Teddy had to say for himself. Would something come of it?

"I'm a wreck," Lorie said. "I didn't mean to screw up."

"Thornberry will take you home," Flint said. She was still choked at the waitress for holding back, but she couldn't take her frustrations out on others. "Take care."

"I'm fine. Don't worry about me." Lorie stood up without warning.

"Are you sure?" Thornberry asked.

"Yeah." Pressing the heels of her palms against her eyes, Lorie shut out the threatening tears, and then walked out the door.

This time the gait was broken momentarily as if the waitress had stopped to catch her breath. The detectives knew it really was to steel herself, to move forward, one step at a time.

"It's hard not to feel sorry for her. To have your dreams within reach, and then snatched away like that." Thornberry snapped her fingers. She caught sight of the pained look on Flint's face. "I shouldn't have said that..."

"Never mind." Flint rubbed at her forehead.

An odd sort of friction sprang up between the detectives. Flint leaned forward and flipped through a folder to pass the time, thinking of her lost dreams. She pushed back what was and contemplated what could be. With Dale. A small smile formed on her lips.

It was the invitation that Thornberry needed. She jumped at the chance to strike up a conversation with Flint.

"What's Teddy hiding?"

"I can't imagine," Flint said and drew in a deep breath. "We'll squeeze it out of the weasel."

Thornberry laughed. "I'm sure it's nothing. Our Teddy wouldn't do anything wrong."

"I know that. It makes me wonder sometimes what people are thinking," Flint said. "He should have mentioned it."

A door slammed. Several sets of boots echoed down the hallway, swept past the boardroom, then faded in the direction of the south foyer. Flint stood up, walked over to the open window, and watched the waves wash against the shoreline, almost soundlessly. More people approaching made her turn to the door.

"I can explain," Teddy said as he hurried into the room. He sat down at the table and ran his hand through his hair.

"Really, Teddy. You of all people should know better." Flint moved over to the whiteboard, staring at it, holding in her annoyance. "You knew Stan and kept quiet. Why?"

"You didn't ask. I didn't think it was important."

"Everything is important in a murder investigation," Flint said.

"I haven't seen Stan since college. We ran into each other a few months ago and had a few beers together at the Shark Cave," Teddy said. "I have no idea what he's been up to or who his friends are." He shrugged.

"What did you talk about?"

"His job. How much he liked living here. His parents."

"You didn't reminisce about the old times?" Thornberry asked.

"Sure. The girls. The football games," Teddy said. "I made a mistake. I should have said something."

Flint leaned back in her chair. Hay stood in the doorway, taking it all in but not commenting.

"So, have you anything more to say now?" Flint asked.

"That's all I know." Teddy threw up his hands. "Honest."

"What were you doing at the jewelry store? Were you visiting Stan?" Thornberry asked, dissatisfied with his casual attitude.

"No. I was meeting up with the fire chief for a coffee."

"I see. At the Seabreeze?" Thornberry asked. She leaned an elbow on the table, flipping through her notebook.

"Yeah, but it was closed like I told you earlier," he said. "So we never caught up with each other."

"Then you went back to the fire hall."

"Yeah, that's right," Teddy said.

Thornberry closed her notebook and looked over to the sergeant.

"Let this be a warning to you, Teddy." Flint gave him a long, contemplating look. "Thanks for coming by."

"Sure, Flint. As if I had a choice." He slapped Hay on the back as he left the room. "I'll find my own way back, partner."

"Take it easy," Hay said. He stepped into the room and sat down.

"What now?" Thornberry asked.

"Time to go home," Flint said, staring out the window to the darkening sky. "We'll pore over everything we have tomorrow. One last time."

Something was out of place she thought. One detail that she had missed. She grew motionless, trying to follow the trail.

Thornberry followed her gaze, wondering what was bothering Flint.

A huge rumble made her start. The gathering clouds had let loose a torrent of rain.

Chapter 27

Jarrett dressed in casual slacks and a sport shirt with no tie, knowing he was likely going to be assigned to his desk for weeks. A sudden movement sent a jolt down the back of his shoulder that stopped him cold. After a few deep breaths, he figured he wouldn't fight hanging out in the office. He strode slowly down the sidewalk to work, enjoying the sun on his face and the song of birds twittering a new morning.

There were no vehicles in the parking lot when he arrived at the station. A glance at his watch confirmed he wasn't too early, but it was strange he was the first one in. He unlocked the front door and headed to his office. The in-box on his desk was overflowing with notices and bulletins. He stepped back to the doorway and listened. There was not a sound, apart from some music playing softly somewhere close by. Jarrett walked down the hallway to the boardroom, to the source of the melody. He threw open the door and was greeted with a flash of light and loud shouts.

Streamers, balloons, and white paper doves hung from the ceiling, twisting lazily in the warm breeze wafting in through the open windows. The detectives, along with a dozen uniformed police officers, stood around the room. Jarrett glanced at all the people, his eyes landing on the large cake with its chocolate message.

'He took one for the team.'

"Way to go Jarrett," one officer shouted. A chorus of congrats and encouragement ensued, everybody talking at once.

If the surprise welcome left Jarrett speechless, he was even more taken aback by all the heartfelt concern for his well-being.

"I'm glad you're back," Flint said. She watched the emotions flicker across the constable's face.

Jarrett was too flabbergasted to say anything, so he took it all in with a grin. Best wishes for a speedy recovery. A few jokes. A playful jab at his good shoulder. But soon the party was over, glasses clinked and cake eaten. The officers streamed out of the boardroom, heading back to their workstations, leaving Jarrett standing awkwardly, an armful of folders still tightly tucked under his arm.

"You can sit down now," Thornberry said in a light cheery voice.

Jarrett plopped down in a chair, tossing his items on the table. He rubbed at his shoulder.

"Is your shoulder okay?" Thornberry asked. "Are you sure you should be back at work?"

"Don't worry about me." He let his hand slip down his arm, resting on his forearm.

"Okay, guys. The fun is over. Are you okay to stay on this with us, Jarrett?"

"Yeah."

"Okay, listen up. We'll have one more go at it, and then?" Flint looked around. "Any thoughts?"

The conversation was sporadic. Not much to say. The case was dead in the water, and they all knew it.

"You still smell from the garbage bin," Jarrett said to his buddy.

"Asshole."

"Is that it then?" Flint said after they had gone on for a number of hours. She ran her hand over the murder book.

"Lunch would be a good idea," Thornberry said as she grinned. "Why am I always the one to suggest that?"

"Rest assured, that's pretty well the best idea we've had all morning," Flint said. "Where should we go?"

They all stood up at the same time, ready to clear their heads and unfreeze their sore butts.

Jarrett sprung up, dropping several folders, papers flying out everywhere and floating softly to the ground. One, brown in colour, caught his eye.

"Oh, shit. I forgot this was addressed to you, Thornberry. It was on my desk when I got in this morning," Jarrett said and handed her a large manila envelope.

"What is it?" Thornberry asked. She looked at the seal on the label. "It's the synopsis. That was fast." Thornberry passed it over to the sergeant. "All yours, boss."

Flint sat back down, reached for a paperknife from the pencil box in the middle of the table and slit open the package. She scanned through a few pages, and then stopped suddenly. Her complexion turned ashen, and her smile vanished.

"What's the matter?" Thornberry asked, peering at the sheet. "Oh my God. Could it be–"

"Stop," Flint shouted, raising both palms outward. The force of her outburst was frightening. The constables glanced at one another, unsure of what had just happened.

Hay was about to speak, but the corporal shook her head. The silence lengthened as they waited to hear what had startled their boss so profoundly.

Flint pushed her hair away from her forehead. After a few moments, she looked up and studied the team perched on their chairs, ready for what was coming next. She knew they weren't ready, she certainly wasn't. Questions whirled through her head with a mind-numbing intensity. Not only would this bombshell send shock waves through the community, but it had a personal implication for her. A hard truth that was troubling. She stared at the page, at the neatly typed sheet. It was there in black and white, no reason to deny it.

Finally, the sergeant spit it out, as quickly and painlessly as she could. "It's Dale. Our Dale." Flint paused to take a deep breath. "My Dale."

"What, the fire chief?" Jarrett shook his head, confusion in his eyes.

"He's the shooter?" Thornberry asked.

"No way," Hay said.

"Okay. Let's settle down," Flint said, regaining her composure, although her face was still white and her lips devoid of any colour. She placed her hand on the folder lightly. "We already know that Stan Kingston received a non-conviction for his DUI last year. But this shows…"

One of the constables coughed.

"Someone died."

"Who?" Several voices rang out at once.

"His wi– Dale's wife," Flint stammered, a trace of sadness clearly audible in her strained voice. She took another deep breath, struggling to continue. She stared out the window, the motion of the ocean, the smell of the salty air always constant, always peaceful to her even when it rolled with fury.

The team sat stunned. The stillness in the room excruciating.

Flint ran her finger down the page. Two simple words struck terror in her heart. She opened her mouth, gasping for air. Momentary panic seized her. Two simple words that made her understand all that had happened. She squeezed her eyes but couldn't stop the tears. They burned as they slid down her cheeks. She looked up with mournful eyes, still watery with tears.

"A child," Flint said. "A child died, as well. Dale's daughter. Sophie." She swiped her hand over her mouth.

Hay turned away and stared at the whitecaps and scudding clouds.

"Should we bring him in?" Thornberry asked, her eyes averted from Flint's pain.

"Jarrett and I will go get him." Hay brought his gaze back to the sergeant. "I'm sorry, Flint."

Flint nodded her head.

The two constables slipped unobtrusively out of the boardroom and hurried down the hallway. The front entrance door closed with a crash. Nobody caring. The echo faded away before Thornberry spoke.

"How did Stan get away with that? He killed two people with his vehicle while in a drunken stupor. And what? They let him go."

"It's a sad fact of life. It happens more often than we would like to think. That's how MADD, Mothers Against Drunk Driving, got started. There wasn't enough accountability," Flint said. As an afterthought, she added, "Still isn't, it appears."

"So Dale, what, just took matters into his own hands? Unbelievable," Thornberry said. "What a stupid thing to do. In his position in the community. Holy shit."

"I get it," Flint said sombrely. "I'm not sure I wouldn't do the same."

"Really?" Thornberry asked. "No you wouldn't. I don't believe that."

"Your only child. Yeah. I can see it. Not saying it's right. But I can certainly understand. If I think about Paige." And already having lost Martin, she thought.

"I suppose."

"When you have children, you'll feel differently," Flint said.

Thornberry shrugged. "What are you going to do about, you know, your relationship?" She winced slightly and glanced regretfully down at her hands. "Sorry. None of my business."

"That's okay. Obviously, I'm done with him." Flint stood up and walked over to the whiteboard. She paused momentarily, then erased everything. After taking down the photos, she sat on the window ledge to wait. The only sounds were the gentle breeze rustling the blinds and the scratching of a pen on a notepad as her corporal scribbled away madly. An hour passed by, and Flint remained at her post. An occasional moan made Thornberry look up.

Hearing voices in the entrance hall, Flint hastily returned to her chair at the end of the long table as far away as she could manage from where Dale would be asked to sit.

Flint wasn't totally certain how he would react to her presence, but she had no option except to see it through. One thing she did know – in the end he wouldn't deny it, probably happy to relieve himself of the pent-up stress. The pressure of losing his family. The horrific act he had committed to revenge his loss. He would be a broken man.

Most murderers were despicable people. This was the first, and only one Flint had even remotely liked. Maybe she even loved him. She took a deep breath and looked up as the constables stepped into the room with Dale in between them. No handcuffs. This was a casual interview as far as the fire chief knew, although he must have suspected something deeper than a chat was afoot.

As Flint locked eyes with him across the room, she saw the hurt. It told her all she needed to know. He knew what was coming down the pipeline.

They settled into chairs, each one with their own thoughts. Thornberry switched on the recorder and announced who was in the room. She glanced at the sergeant, then started the inquiry.

"Do you wish to have a lawyer present?" Thornberry asked.

"Yes, I think I better." His voice was meek, his face crumpling into resignation. "Am I under arrest?"

"Yes, we're charging you with the murder of Stan Kingston."

Flint's heart stopped beating.

Even the blinds had ceased their relentless rattling.

Chapter 28

Thornberry got the warrant for Dale Begley's house within the hour and the search began. The forensics team took the upstairs while the two detectives combed through the ground floor rooms. Flint had a pretty good idea where to look. She went into the study where she had often sat reading with a glass of Pinot while Dale did some paperwork. She headed straight for the oak desk and rummaged around the underside of a pullout shelf until her fingers touched the cool metal. A creak at the door made her turn. Thornberry stood in the doorway, her brow furrowed with worry.

Flint inserted the key in the bottom drawer and slowly pulled on the brass handle. She picked up the small wooden box and placed it on the desktop. After a moment's hesitation, she unclasped the case and lifted up the lid. The gun had a royal blue finish with hardwood checkered grips, gold medallions in each panel. She stared down at the Colt Python .357 magnum revolver, then closed the lid.

"It's a beauty," Thornberry said. "From the 1970s."

"Yeah, it is. But more importantly, it's chambered to shoot a .38 special," Flint said and sighed. "I've seen it before."

Thornberry remained silent.

"Dale loves this gun," Flint whispered before she felt she would be overtaken by tears once again.

The quiet was broken by a set of footsteps that had landed at the door.

"Sorry, ladies." Ryan stepped into the room and approached the detectives.

"This is what we're looking for," Flint said and handed him the box. "It's the murder weapon."

"Okay. I'll put a rush on it." He placed it into an evidence bag and looked at the sergeant.

"Yeah. We don't need to drag this one out any longer than necessary," Flint said. She closed the drawer softly and stood up.

"The blood sample from Dale is already at the lab. I have my best man on it. Give him a few hours."

"Thanks for everything."

"Are you okay?" Ryan asked, placing a hand on Flint's shoulder.

"I will be." Flint thought she would scream the next time someone asked her that.

* * *

Dale Begley lay flat on the thin mattress, a pillow under his head and a worn blanket covering his chilled body. He closed his eyes, feeling nothing but emptiness. The first heavy drops of rain splattered onto the window high up on the wall. It was an oddly comforting sound in an otherwise bleak atmosphere. A jangle of keys alerted him to the moment.

Constable Hay entered the cell.

Dale sat up, but he couldn't look the man in the eye, overcome with shame. Revenge was a double-edged sword. He had lost something to gain something else.

* * *

Hay escorted Dale to an interview room where the detectives had set up. He sat on a chair in the hallway. His job was to be vigilant of any trouble that might arise. He would have to do it alone because Jarrett had booked off with his bad shoulder before even putting in a full day of work.

A conventional looking gentleman dressed in a light grey suit with white shirt and a striped tie rounded the corner and stopped in front of the constable.

"Mr. Henderson?" Hay asked.

"Yes."

"In here." Hay rapped on the door lightly and the lawyer entered the room.

* * *

Mr. Henderson was greeted cordially by the detectives. After seating himself next to his client, he placed his briefcase on the table and pulled out a fresh pad of paper, along with a gold pen. He turned and looked Dale up and down, taking in the rumpled clothes and unkempt hair, knowing this was going to be rough.

Dale glanced in his direction for a second then returned his attention to his hands. His face and neck were moist and reeked of stale sweat.

"Could I have a few moments with my client? Won't be long."

"No problem," Thornberry said.

The detectives shuffled out of the room, closing the door behind them.

"I feel sorry for him," Hay said.

Flint's phone pinged. She answered, listened, and then hung up.

"That was the lab. It's confirmed. Dale's DNA matched the blood at the crime scene." Flint sighed. "But we knew it would."

"Is he going to confess?" Hay asked. He motioned them over and gestured to the bench along the wall.

"We found the gun," Flint said, ignoring the question.

"Did it–" Hay stopped when the door opened.

"Okay." The lawyer stood half in and half out of the room. He looked about ready to say more, then thought better of it and spun on his heels.

Hay picked up his cellphone and continued with his video game, keeping one eye on the door.

In the few minutes the detectives had been gone, two things had changed. Dale's complexion had turned a sickly pale grey close to the colour of his lawyer's suit, and the glass in front of him was empty. He licked his chapped lips with his tongue over and over.

Flint stuck her head out the door and spoke to Hay. She stood there until he returned. He handed her the glass jug. Its coolness felt nice, the water droplets on the outside surface sliding onto her warm hand. She placed the pitcher on the table and sat down without speaking. Dale acknowledged her kind gesture with a nod, keeping his gaze lowered.

Thornberry punched the recorder button to begin the interrogation.

"Okay, I would like to start with some background information," the corporal said.

"Sure," Dale answered.

"Where did you live before you moved to Castlecrest?"

"Vancouver." Dale stared at his hands in his lap.

"For how long?"

"Five years."

"What did you do there?"

"I was deputy fire chief in New Westminster. It's an outlying suburb."

"That's a good job. Why did you move back here?" Thornberry used a pencil to scribble any thoughts that came to her as she questioned Dale.

"This is my hometown. I was offered the fire chief job by Flint's father... by Victor Sullivan." He greedily guzzled another glass of water.

"I see," Thornberry said. "You were married and had a child."

"Yes." He visibly flinched at the mention of his family but continued after an imperceptible pause. "Sophie."

"Why did you keep that a secret?"

"I don't know." Dale shrugged.

"They were both killed by a drunk driver."

"Yes. In a crosswalk." Dale spoke softly. His eyes glazed over, tears threatening.

"Did you shoot Stan Kingston?"

"Don't answer that." Mr. Henderson touched his client's arm. Dale pulled his arm to one side.

After a brief hesitation, Dale said, "Yes, I shot the clerk." He glanced over to Flint who looked away. "The man ran over my wife and my beautiful child. Sophie was only four years old. He got away scot-free." He drew in a breath and let it go. "I went into the jewelry store to buy a bracelet for..." He choked back a sob. "Anyway, I recognized the man as soon as I laid eyes on him. Of course, he didn't know who I was. Just another customer as far as he was concerned. He probably hadn't given me or what he did another thought since he got off. He stood behind the counter, all smiley and pleasant, but all I could think about was he killed my family. I walked out of the store and went home." He stopped abruptly.

The quietness of the room was complete. A single tear fell down his cheek.

"Weren't you supposed to meet up with Teddy at the Seabreeze?" Thornberry asked.

"I was seeing red. I forgot about everything else." Dale lowered his head.

"Why did you go back to the store?"

"I was sitting in my kitchen. The hate for the man was eating me up. I had to go back to the store and confront him. All I wanted was an acknowledgement that he destroyed my life. Maybe an apology. Something, anything. Was that too much to ask?"

Flint felt that his words came from the heart. The sorrow hit deep.

Tears flowed freely now. Dale struggled to go on. "But I got nothing. He wouldn't do it. The man stared at me as if, as if he really didn't give a shit. How can someone be so insensitive? He told me to get the hell out of the store."

Flint looked up. That was the first bad thing anyone had said about Stan, but she believed the fire chief. Stan had hidden his real character well, nobody the wiser.

Dale's breathing became raspy.

"Do you want a break?" Thornberry asked.

"No. I'm fine. I want to get it over with." Dale took another deep breath, holding it for a long moment before he expelled the air. "I took my gun with me. I shot him once. I stumbled against the glass case. It broke, and then I ran. I wasn't even sure he was dead. Immediately, I thought I would regret my actions, but to be honest I didn't. I had already lost everything. Nothing mattered to me anymore."

He stared at Flint who met his eyes for the last time. "I'm so sorry for you. For us." He folded his arms on the table, lowered his head and cried.

* * *

Flint pulled into the driveway as the light faded in the evening sky. The razor thin crescent moon looked dull against the broad sweep of the galaxy stars. The house was dark with only a floor lamp switched on beside where her dad would be poring over a book. He had taken it upon himself to wait up for her no matter what time she rolled in. She looked up to the second story bedroom window and saw the low glow of her daughter's night light.

Paige would ask lots of questions when Dale stopped coming round. But soon he would fade into the background and other things would engage her thoughts. Flint wasn't sure she could forget as easily.

Then there was the community.

Flint slipped in through the back door. The dog lifted his head, bared his teeth in a smile and plopped his head back onto his front paws. She rubbed his ears and walked down the hallway to the living room. Her dad placed his book on the side table. She melted into the softness of the couch, feet up on the coffee table.

"Is it true?"

"Yes." She couldn't meet his eyes.

"It was his decision."

"I know that."

"I hired him as fire chief when I retired. He had it all," her dad said.

They held each other's gaze for a moment, and some silent message went unspoken.

Flint wanted to cry.

"We both cared for him."

"We did." Flint stood up. "Good night, Dad."

"Night, sweetheart." Victor picked up his book and adjusted his glasses.

Flint grabbed the dog on the way out the door. They headed for the edge of the lawn toward the shoreline. She lit up a cigarette, fingering the engraving on the lighter Dale had given her last year when they first started dating. It was a funny gift to give someone in these times. But she was glad, she had something.

Sitting there silently on the rocks, Flint took in the view of the ocean vanishing into infinity, and inhaled the air that carried with it the sharp smell of salt.

Chapter 29

As Flint pulled the comb through her lifeless hair, she leaned into the mirror and sighed. She hoped the concealer she had applied to the ugly bags under her eyes wouldn't give away how much sleep she had not been getting. She stepped outside and heard a rooster crowing in the distance. The light in the early hours of dawn reddened the eastern sky, a hint of a storm coming.

Flint was the only one on the road until a police cruiser rounded a corner on the main drag. The vehicle slowed down, the officer throwing her a wave of recognition. At the station, the outside lights were blinking off. She entered the building and walked along the hallway, glad of the eerie peacefulness.

Flint sat in her office, glancing occasionally out the window. She was finishing up her report when her cell phone pinged. Wearily she glanced at the screen and answered. As she listened, Thornberry strolled in and placed two coffees and a box of croissants on the desk. Flint held up a finger to give her a moment.

Loud voices floated into the room. Both constables stood in the doorway. Flint regarded Jarrett quizzically and gestured them to come in and sit down, phone still glued to her ear. After several more minutes of nodding her head, she hung up.

"I thought you were on leave."

"I am. But I wanted to be here when the case was brought to a close," Jarrett said, "and to say..."

"Never mind that." Flint said, thinking maybe she should take a few weeks off before she went crazy with the outpouring of condolences. It's not as if someone near and dear to her had died. The relationship died. She put on a benevolent smile.

"That was Ryan on the phone. The bullets matched. It's the murder weapon, as we figured. I know Dale confessed to killing Stan, but having solid evidence for the courts makes it easier all round for everyone."

Easier to put it in a closet and forget the whole affair, Flint thought.

A moment of quiet ensued as the team took on the full meaning of what the fire chief had done. Saying it out loud had made it real.

"Why did he keep the gun?" Jarrett asked, breaking into everybody's thoughts.

Thornberry had been sitting and listening, but now she spoke up. "I visited Dale this morning in his cell to clear up a few things. I wasn't sure he would see me, but he wanted to talk. Guess it gets lonely in there. Anyway, that was the first thing I asked him." She looked around the room. "Why not chuck the gun?"

"Well, what did he say?" Jarrett asked, leaning forward in his chair. "Come on."

"Nostalgia," Thornberry said. "It was left to him by his grandfather who passed away last year, someone he looked up to when he was a kid. He said he couldn't toss it away."

"He must have realized it was damning evidence," Jarrett said.

"I suppose. But he really didn't seem to care." Thornberry glanced sideways at Flint.

"Did you ask him about that night in Stan's apartment?" Flint asked, touching her head where the lump had been. "Was it him?"

The constables looked at the sergeant with curiosity, not sure what she was talking about.

"He was looking for the DUI papers, thinking his name would be on them. He didn't mean to knock you down."

"What are you–" Hay stopped when Thornberry gave him a warning glare.

"I see," Flint said.

There was a brief lull in the conversation.

"Why didn't he tell us about his family?" Hay finally asked. "I don't get that."

"That was the first stumbling block. It's like he didn't know why either, except he said since it happened he hadn't been able to find his way forward, no matter what he did. Then he became withdrawn and wouldn't answer any more questions." Thornberry shrugged. "So I left."

"Does anybody have anything else to add?" Flint asked, looking around at her team.

"I hope I get a cuter partner for the next few months," Hay said.

"Someone not as smart as me, so you look clever," Jarrett responded, poking fun at his buddy.

Thornberry chuckled at his joke, but turned away shyly when he smiled at her.

"We seem to have everything wrapped up," Flint said, "except for our reports."

The team let out a collective groan of protest.

Flint held up her hand. "Okay. Take a break today. We'll get back on track tomorrow."

Both Hay and Jarrett popped out of their chairs and split. They strolled down the hallway slowly, gabbing loudly about something. Their voices reverberating back to the detectives. It sounded like a disagreement about sports. Probably hockey or football.

Thornberry reached for another croissant, licking the chocolate off the top before biting into it. "Who doesn't love chocolate?" She looked at Flint. "I'm around later if you want to do something."

"Thanks," Flint said. She could use a friend.

"See you later." Thornberry stood up, glanced at the last croissant and left.

Flint shut down her laptop, closing the lid softly. She leaned back in her chair and crossed her arms. Disembodied laughter floated from the detachment at the other end of the building, followed by boots briskly stomping down the hallway. The sound moved closer, and then abruptly stopped. A man, his large presence framed perfectly in the doorway, was dressed in full uniform. His black hair had a few streaks of grey at the temple.

"Sir." Flint jumped out of her chair.

"Take it easy, Flint." Superintendent Allen Gill stepped into the room and glanced around, his eyes drawn toward the windows. "Nice."

"Yeah."

"Your team did a pretty good job. Exceptional job, really," Gill said, then frowned. "Too bad about the fire chief though. Dale Begley. I've known him a long time. Didn't see that coming."

"Neither did we." Flint tugged self-consciously at a lock of hair, brushing it behind her ear.

Gill shifted his gaze back to the sergeant. "You okay?"

"I'm fine," Flint said. His tone of voice made her think he knew about the fire chief and her. This time she didn't mind the inquiry. He even seemed to care. Was he offering her an olive branch?

"Well, keep it up." Gill swung away, whistling as he strolled back to the south foyer.

Flint sipped her coffee, not aware that it had grown cold. She eyed the last croissant, decided not to and closed the box. The blinds fluttered. She felt a warm breeze on her face and took a breath of the fresh air. Everything will be okay, she thought. Paige and her. Mom and dad. With one last look around her office, she locked the door and headed home.

Everything will be okay.

List of Characters

RCMP Sergeant Marlowe Flint
RCMP Corporal Naomi Thornberry
RCMP Constable Gordon Hay
RCMP Constable Dennis Jarrett
Dr. Kelly Churchman — pathologist from the BC Coroners Service
Ryan Harper — forensic investigator
Arlene — office manager at the RCMP station
Superintendent Hank Parker
Superintendent Allen Gill — acting superintendent
Paula Wilkes — owner of the Seabreeze Café
Lorie Sanders — waitress
Kyle Ingram — cook
Tim — kitchen hand
Rick — kitchen hand
Dale Begley — fire chief
Edward Ewert (Teddy) — fireman
Ben Altman — owner of Altman Jewelry and Diamonds
Stan Kingston — jewelry store assistant
Percy Kingston — Stan's brother
Victor Sullivan — Flint's father
Oleane Sullivan — Flint's mother

Paige — Flint's daughter
Bodhi — Flint's dog
Mrs. Shaver — bank manager
Tanya — receptionist at the bank
Casey Snider — drifter
Kevin and Paul — guys at the bar
Ronald and Marianne — owners of Sports Unlimited
George and Agnes — owners of the men's clothing store
Mr. Glanford — owner of the pharmacy
Mrs. Hamilton — owner of the rooming house
Peter — kid at the community centre

If you enjoyed this book, please let others know by leaving a quick review on Amazon. Also, if you spot anything untoward in the paperback, get in touch. We strive for the best quality and appreciate reader feedback.

editor@thebookfolks.com

Also by Kathy Garthwaite

Inspector Gibson cuts short a jaunt in his beloved kayak to attend a murder inquiry. The investigation soon meets a brick wall, but he suspects the victim's co-workers are involved. He must act quickly before the case, like the weather, goes cold.

The veteran detective is flown out to the east of the country to help set up a major crimes task force. He soon has a murder on his hands when a local shopkeeper is found dead on the beach. Estranged from his melancholic wife, Gibson's loyalties become divided.

When a woman is murdered, Inspector William Gibson immediately suspects her husband is responsible. His junior partner is not so sure. But when the truth emerges it has a knock-on effect that will change the detective's life for ever. And not in a good way.

Sign up to our mailing list to find out about new releases and special offers!

www.thebookfolks.com

Manufactured by Amazon.ca
Bolton, ON

14911250R00114